SEVENTEEN PRAYERS TO THE MANY-EYED MOTHER

Stories by
Eliza Victoria

avenida

Published by:
19th Avenida Publishing House
Imus City, Cavite
myavenida.com
avenidabooks@gmail.com

avenida f /myavenidaph

First printed May 2022, Philippines

ISBN 978-621-8264-11-3

1 3 5 7 9 10 8 6 4 2

This book is a work of fiction. Any similarities to existing persons (living or dead), places, icons, or institutions, are purely coincidental, or were used in the pursuit of creative excellence.

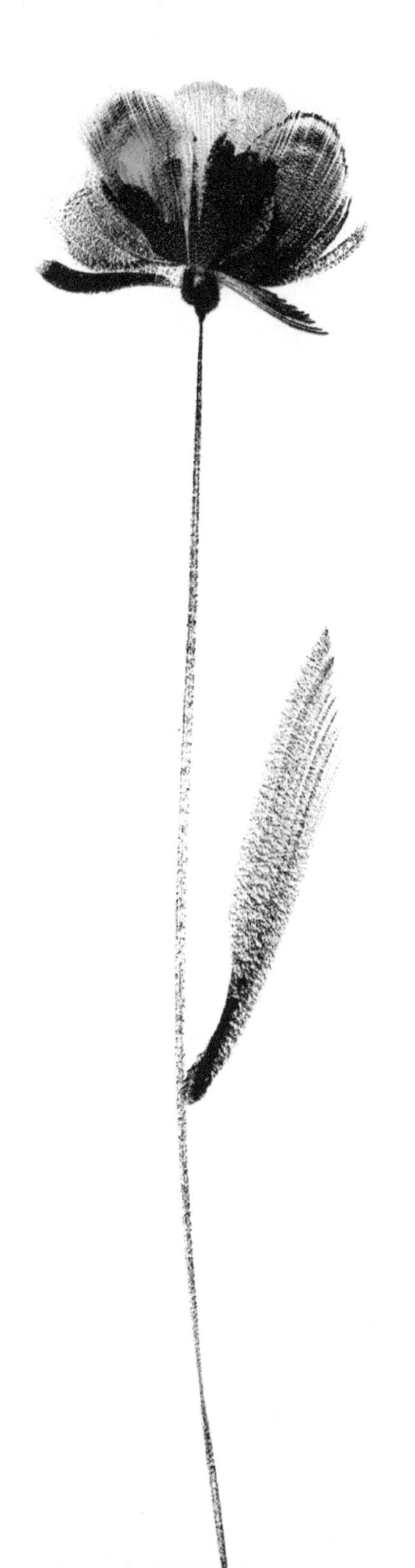

TABLE OF CONTENTS

CARPE NOCTEM

"Your name is really Michelle Pfeiffer Santos?"

Michelle smiled and folded her hands on her lap,
then placed them on the table, then placed them back on
her lap. She didn't quite know what to do with her hands.

"You must be sick of hearing that, aren't you?" said
Tara, who looked thinner than her LinkedIn profile photo.
Tall, model-thin, every hair strand in place. Michelle wore
mascara for the first time today, and her lashes felt like
they weighed a ton.

"It's a good conversation starter," Michelle said. Tara
glanced up to throw her a quick smile before returning
to Michelle's CV with furrowed brows. They were in
the startup's office, a co-working space in Sheung Wan.
Bright-red tables. Micro-roasted coffee. A 3D printer. I
could get used to this, Michelle thought, and was suffused
with excitement that made her palms sweat.

"I heard that 'Tara' means 'hill' or 'elevated place'
in Gaelic," Michelle said. "It's the Anglicised version of

'Teamhair', a sacred hill in Ireland where the high kings lived."

"Really?" Tara said. But Michelle could tell Tara's response was coming from another continent. Something's wrong, but Michelle pushed the thought away and focused on the trinkets on Tara's desk: a syringe pen, a gumball dispenser shaped like a basketball court, a candy tin marked Women Empowermints.

"See," Michelle said, "that's way cooler than, 'I'm named after the actress in *The Fabulous Baker Boys*.'"

"That's your Michelle Pfeiffer reference?" Tara said, laughing. "Not *Batman Returns*?"

Michelle had not actually seen *The Fabulous Baker Boys*, but she was in too deep. She just smiled and shrugged.

"I like you, Michelle," Tara said. "I really do. May I ask, who set up this appointment? Was it Paul?"

"Yes."

"I see here that your address is in Manila. You were interviewed online?"

"That's right."

"Did Paul interview you?"

"Daniel," Michelle said.

"Daniel's on leave." Tara bit her lower lip, thinking. "Did Daniel ask if you have managerial experience?"

"No," Michelle said, and already she could feel the excitement ebbing away.

"I see here that you don't," Tara said. "I'm so sorry, Michelle, there must have been a terrible miscommunication. The position that's open right now calls for at least eight years of managerial experience.

Magazine or newspaper editor, that sort of thing. We need someone to be captain of the ship, so to speak. We're still building out the writing pool, but once we open up those positions, I'll make sure to give you a call. How does that sound? Oh my God." Tara placed her hands on her cheeks. "You didn't come all the way here just for the interview, did you? Please tell me you're on vacation and this was just a line in your itinerary."

For some strange reason, Michelle didn't want to hurt Tara's feelings, even though her legs had turned to jelly, even though she could feel the burn of tears in the corner of her eyes. "Oh, no," she said with a wave of her hand, *Don't be silly.* "No, no. I've been meaning to visit Hong Kong, and when Daniel said he'd set up an interview with the CEO"—*and that I'm "a good fit"*—"I thought, why not drop by, the office is connected to the MTR anyway." She blinked once, twice. "Your office is very nice."

"I will definitely have a long and serious talk with Daniel." Tara opened and looked through several drawers before finally taking out a red and black envelope. "Listen, I want you to have a good time in Hong Kong. I got this ticket for a walking tour this afternoon. Comes with snacks. Please go if you're free?"

"Oh, you don't have to—"

"Please," Tara said, placing the envelope in front of her. "I insist." She smiled. "I'll keep your CV on file, okay?"

THE HOSTEL RECEPTION desk was tended that day by a woman in her eighties with a diamond brooch on her lapel above her inscrutable name pin, and a large burn scar from her right cheek down to her neck. She was probably the hostel manager. Or owner. When Michelle entered the lobby, the woman was feeding the fish in the large aquarium sitting on the table behind the desk. On the wall next to her were framed photos, handwritten notes, newspaper clippings—a wall-sized scrapbook page. Michelle could only read the headlines in English:

PACIFIC BATTLE WIDENS. MANILA AREA BOMBED. JAPANESE FORCES ATTACK HONG KONG. 1,689 DEFENDERS CAPTURED BY JAPS AS GARRISON FALLS. HONG KONG SURRENDERS.

The woman looked up, smiled at her, and greeted her in Cantonese. "Hello," Michelle said, and left right after, not wanting to mangle "Máahnseuhng hóu", having already reached her quota of crippling shame for the day.

She enjoyed hostel rooms. Crisp linen, fluffy towels, the small bottles of face cream, perfume, and lotion, which she lined up now on her bedside table as she sat on the bed and cried. Her fingers accidentally pushed the lotion out of line because they shook with her every sob. *Get ahold of yourself.* Michelle swiped an arm across her face and connected her phone to the WiFi, shook out her clothes from her backpack, went through the little rituals that steadied her, that gave her a semblance of order.

The first email that came in was from her boss back in Manila with the subject: We need to talk ASAP.

No one knew she was here, and she was glad for that. At least no one knew she had drained her meager savings into a trip that she thought would result in a better-paying job. With only herself involved, the guilt and disappointment could be easily bottled up and pushed deep into a dark corner, like a pair of jeans that no longer fit. Easy-peasy. Same as always.

THE WALKING TOUR began on Electric Road, and Michelle tried to enjoy it ("This road used to be nameless, until Hong Kong Electric built a power plant—"), tried to enjoy the humid air, the tourists jostling for a photo, the droplets of moisture falling from the air-conditioning units jutting out of the buildings they passed. Someone— someone who presumably neglected to read the brochure— raised his hand and asked about the Battle of Hong Kong.

"We have a different guided tour for that," the tour guide said, but went on to talk about it anyway: the unexpected attack, the heavy artillery fire, the Japanese troops landing in then British-ruled Hong Kong with an order to take no prisoners, the massacres, the doomed defense. The air raids and bombings that severed water mains, and the Japanese taking control of key reservoirs, threatening inhabitants with death by thirst. Hong Kong surrendered after 18 days, on Christmas Day of 1941.

To Michelle's surprise, the woman standing next to her said, "Tragedies follow the same pattern, if you observe them long enough. Hitler's Germany attacked Stalin's Soviet Union and blocked food and supplies from entering Leningrad for 872 days, leading to famine that wiped out a million people. Famine also overtook the city of Bari when Norman forces blockaded the Byzantine stronghold. Spartans destroyed the Athenian navy and implemented a sea blockade, slowly starving Athens, which was unable to reach its vessels to import grain. Time stretches out like the ocean. You see the patterns in the waves once you step away."

They started walking again, and that was when Michelle turned to take a good look at the woman. She was Michelle's height, but a bit older. Late twenties. Pretty, and aware of it too, based on the way she held herself, the way she lifted her chin, the way she walked. *Aren't you glad you're in the presence of beauty?* The kind of confidence that both intimidated Michelle and made her roll her eyes.

"Well, it's the individual lives you can't predict," Michelle said, "which makes them more interesting."

The woman smiled. And what a brilliant smile, as though she were a child hiding under a table, and Michelle had just lifted up a corner of the tablecloth and found her there.

"That's right," she said. "That is absolutely right. You tend to forget that."

The last stop was at the Tin Hau Temple in Yau Ma Tei, a shrine dedicated to the goddess of the sea. Before massive land reclamation, the tour guide said, the shrine was located on the waterfront, where fishermen prayed for safe voyage. As it was the last stop, the tour guide bade everyone goodbye and wished the tourists a safe journey back to their respective accommodations. A number of the walking tour participants followed her inside the temple, leaving Michelle alone with Ms Tragedies-Follow-the-Same-Pattern.

"You're not going in?" she asked Michelle now.

"I always feel weird stepping inside places of worship as a tourist," Michelle said. "I would not be going in there to pray. I'd just be looking. And there are people praying in there, and I'd be looking at them and at the shrines like they're all museum pieces. It just feels disrespectful."

The woman smiled. "You can pray, you know," she said. "In your own way."

"Maybe," Michelle said. She waved goodbye and left.

THIRTY MINUTES OF getting lost and two aching feet later, Michelle was clutching on to her rapidly depleting stockpile of silver linings. Hong Kong had better public transportation and traffic conditions than Manila, but she might as well be walking down Ayala Avenue again, past shops she couldn't afford. She stopped by a stall on the road and asked the old man running it if he sold water. He couldn't understand her, and the stream of Cantonese he screamed her way sounded like bitter rejection, and left her with a feeling of shame that surprised her with its intensity. When she finally reached the Tsim Sha Tsui Promenade, she sat on a bench with a groan and stared at the neon-outlined buildings of the city skyline and at their reflections in the water below. The view was stunning, and she was reminded of Tara again. *You didn't come all the way here just for the interview, did you?*

I thought I was going to have all of this, Michelle thought, staring at the lights across the water.

Someone sat next to her and waved a plastic bottle in front of her face. "Water?" It was the woman from the walking tour.

"You again?" Michelle said. She took a long drink and wiped her mouth. "Thank you. You have no idea how much I needed that."

They stared at the buildings in silence for a moment.

"Are you waiting for the Symphony of Lights?" the woman asked.

"Yes," Michelle said. "But right now I'm mostly trying to keep my feet from dying."

"I like the skyline," the woman said. "But I think the Symphony of Lights is overrated."

"Wow," Michelle said, who was in fact looking forward to the light and sound show. "You should apply as an ambassador."

The woman laughed. After a brief silence, Michelle asked, "What's your name?"

"Brenda," she said nonchalantly, as though she'd just plucked the name from thin air. "You?"

"Sarah," Michelle said.

Brenda snorted, as though she knew, as though she were in on the joke.

"So, *Sarah*," Brenda said, "what brings you to Hong Kong?"

She sighed. "I thought I was going to be offered a job."

"What do you do back home?"

"I'm a secretary," Michelle said. "I write memos, handle the office budget. Stuff like that."

Brenda glanced at her. "You look like a college student. It's your first job?"

"Yes."

"And you want a change of scenery."

"You can say that," Michelle said. "Because I am going to get fired."

"Oh?"

"Five months ago, I had to pay the bills after my mother got hospitalised," she said. She had never told anyone this. But perhaps it made sense, confessing to a complete stranger she would never meet again. "I couldn't pay my rent, and my mother needed money for her maintenance medication. I needed cash right away, and I was desperate, so I took some money from the office petty cash. I was going to give it back after payday. Which I did. But the next month, I got strapped for cash again, and took money again." *We need to talk ASAP.* "Now I think my boss knows what I've been doing."

Brenda said nothing.

"I just want to stay here," she said. "Hide here. Change my name."

"What if you found out you would die tomorrow?" Brenda asked. "I bet all these problems would seem so small."

"I know it's just money," Michelle said. "But what can I do? I won't die tomorrow. That's the problem. So I have years ahead of me to carry this problem and worry about money, money, money." She sighed again. "I'm so tired of worrying about the little things. I wish I could worry about the bigger things."

"Like the meaning of life?"

She laughed. "Yes, that's a good start."

Brenda handed her two incense sticks.

"I got that from the temple of Tin Hau," Brenda said. "Good night, Michelle."

She was already halfway through the light and sound show when she realised that Brenda had called her by her real name.

BACK IN HER hostel room, Michelle took out the remaining bills from her purse. Brenda's incense sticks fell on the bed. She paused for a moment, regarding them as if they were sticks of dynamite. How did Brenda know her name? Did Michelle tell her? Did the tour guide hand out leaflets with the participants' names? She pushed the incense sticks under the pillows and looked for a movie to watch on cable.

MICHELLE WAS SITTING next to Brenda on a bench at the Tsim Sha Tsui Promenade. Except that it couldn't be the Promenade, because the lights and the buildings were gone, and the calm of Victoria Harbour was replaced by a roiling ocean, salt water waves crashing against the harbor railing. Michelle felt the spray on her face, tasted the salt in the corner of her mouth.

The waves slammed against the railing like a slap. Michelle sat up with a jolt. "Your name's not Brenda," she said. *And this is not the Promenade. And that is not Victoria Harbour.*

Brenda smiled and handed her one long-stemmed flower, its black petals veined with red.

"You can pray, you know," she said. "In your own way."

Michelle took the flower. What? she wanted to ask, but somehow she knew what she wanted to do. She stood and approached the harbor railing, slowly, as if the ocean behind it were a wild beast she didn't want to provoke.

She climbed over the railing. Somehow she knew she would not drown, that the edge of the water would reach only her ankles. She waded into the water, her toes tunnelling into the mud.

Is any of this worth it? she thought. What will be the end of all this, all this working, all this hoping, all this living?

She placed the flower on top of the water and watched it bob and then disappear beneath an approaching wave. The wave was higher than any building on the Promenade, higher than any building she had ever seen.

MICHELLE AWOKE AND lifted her head. A movie she didn't recognize was playing on the TV. Her pillows felt damp. She pushed them aside.

The incense sticks were missing. In their place was one long-stemmed flower, its black petals veined with red.

SHE DISTINCTLY REMEMBERED receiving the incense sticks from Brenda at the Promenade, felt their shape in the palm of her hand.

And yet—

Michelle meant to throw the flower in the trash, but changed her mind at the last minute and dropped it in the bathroom sink.

I am losing my mind.

"I just need to sleep," she told her reflection, and stepped out of the bathroom.

Brenda was sitting on the edge of the bed.

Michelle froze, too shocked to scream.

"Hello, Michelle," Brenda said, lifting up a bouquet of flowers. The petals were a soft, pale pink at the base, white at the tip. "These come from the garden where you die two years from now, at the age of twenty-two."

In her mind, Michelle burst through the hostel room door and ran down ten flights of stairs to the MTR. In reality, she only managed to enter the bathroom again and lock the door behind her. She sat on the floor, hugging her knees, and only then saw and felt the mud between her bare toes.

"Michelle," Brenda said from the other side of the door.

Michelle wanted to scream but couldn't.

"Why are you afraid? You asked for this, didn't you?"

What? But already Michelle was standing up, hands hovering over the doorknob.

"You wanted to know the end of all this," Brenda said. "You have prayed, in your own way, but not to Tin Hau, not to Aman Sinaya, not to Haik, not to Poseidon. You asked the question to someone older."

Michelle opened the bathroom door. "Your name is not Brenda."

Brenda handed her the bouquet of flowers, gently, as if it were an infant.

"My true name is old, too old for your ears and for your tongue," she said. "The Ancient Ocean's true name is older still."

Michelle felt as if she were being handed wisdom too deep and destructive for her to receive. "I will die in a garden in two years?" The flowers smelled sweet, like syrup.

"Follow me," Brenda said.

STEPPING OUT OF the hostel's back doors should have led them to a patio, where guests went to smoke or drink, but here suddenly was a cobblestone path, reminding Michelle of Calle Crisologo in Vigan. On the left, right next to Brenda, was a river, loud as a waterfall, as though it had swollen after a downpour. She wouldn't want to be caught in that current. It looked swift and fierce enough to kill.

"This is Calle Tiempo," Brenda said as they walked. "That is not its true name, just a name you understand. The river beside it flows and pours into the Ancient Ocean. As we all do."

"Where does this path lead?"

"To a place where all that have died still live," Brenda said. "Where dead languages are still spoken. Coptic. Akkadian. Even Sainte, a short-lived language invented by ten children who joined the Children's Crusade, before they drowned together in the Mediterranean Sea." She turned to Michelle. "Omnia vivunt."

The cobblestone path opened up on a golden-lit square. She followed Brenda into a restaurant with checked tablecloths and peeling white paint. The sign only said Café Tempus, but the place reminded Michelle of Café Leona, a restaurant named after the Ilocano poet, where she had bagnet for the first time. *Pork belly deep-fried more than once*, the server had said, *for maximum crispiness and maximum damage.*

"After I graduated," she said when they were seated, "I went to Ilocos Sur with a group of friends."

Brenda looked around, delighted. "It is a fond memory."

"I had fun on that trip," Michelle said. No more papers to write. No more exams to take. No more worries, at least for a brief moment. "Everything felt..." She paused, thinking of the right word. "Everything felt possible." She laughed, embarrassed. "But that was a long time ago."

The server—who somehow looked like that jolly server from long ago, a short, stout man with a booming laugh, completely normal, definitely not the kind of person who would whip out a bouquet of flowers taken from a person's hour of death—served them a plate of bagnet with vinegar, a plate of leafy greens, two bowls of rice, and two iced teas.

"For maximum crispiness and maximum damage," Brenda said. "Let's eat." After a moment's silence, Brenda said, "Michelle."

"Yes?" She looked up from her food and Brenda was holding the black flower she had given her—

By Victoria Harbour. Except it wasn't Victoria Harbour, was it?

"This is Carpe Noctem," Brenda said. "Again, not its real name, just a name you understand. It grows on the banks of the river."

Michelle set aside the cutlery and folded her hands on her lap, then placed them on the table, then placed them back on her lap.

"Everything felt possible then, you said," Brenda continued. "But you don't feel this way anymore. What if I offer you a chance to open all of these paths? Time stretches out like the ocean. You see the patterns in the waves once you step away. What if I can give you the power to step away?"

Michelle met her gaze. Brenda placed the flower on the table between them.

"Outside of time," she said, "the first word ever spoken can still be heard, alongside the last word that will ever be spoken. Wouldn't you like to know what they are?"

Michelle gulped.

"You're afraid," Brenda said.

Michelle nodded.

"I understand," Brenda said. "This is the appropriate reaction to a knowledge this terrible and precious."

Michelle took a deep breath. "Can I ask you a question?"

"Yes. Anything."

"Were you ever," she said, pointing at her chest, gesturing around her head, "were you ever once like me?"

Brenda squinted. "Mortal? Human? No."

Michelle considered this. "So," she said, nodding at the red-veined flower, "if I accept this, I will—"

"You will become transcendent," Brenda said.

Silence.

"Wow," Michelle murmured.

"Wow," Brenda echoed. She sat back. "You are refusing my offer."

"Do I need to decide now? This is very short notice. I just met you!"

"So you choose to continue to follow the path that will end with you dying in the garden in two years?"

"The destination could change," Michelle said. "Right? I want to see where it goes."

"I have seen the waves, the patterns. All of your paths end the same way."

Michelle nodded to herself, sniffed, tried to finish her bagnet. After a minute she dropped her spoon and cried into her hands.

Brenda sounded chastened. "Michelle—"

"Why would you tell me this?" she said, her breath hitching. "I didn't need to know this!"

Brenda pushed the napkin holder closer. "Because I am selfish," she said. "Because I am lonely. Because I would like a companion to walk with me outside of time, and to walk with me when I step into the river."

Michelle stopped sobbing. She wiped her face. Here, finally, a sentiment she could understand.

"Let's just finish dinner, okay?" she said.

BRENDA WALKED HER back on the cobblestone path she called Calle Tiempo.

"So nothing is ever lost?" Michelle said.

"Nothing is ever lost."

"Then maybe I shouldn't be so sad that I will be dead in two years," Michelle said. She felt a revelation rising within her like a tangible object, brushing against her edges. She felt it in her chest, in her throat. A sentiment she could not completely articulate: I should have lived like the Michelle sitting years ago in Café Leona, golden-lit and grateful and open-hearted.

"You still live in time," Brenda said. "That is your curse."

Michelle looked at her. "Say something in Sainte."

Brenda took a deep breath and said a few words. One of them ended with what sounded to Michelle like vyan-dre.

"What does that mean?"

She stopped walking and drew Michelle close for an embrace. Behind Brenda, the river's current rushed past.

"Forgive me," Brenda said. "You are right. All is not known to me. All the paths I've seen, they end with you in that garden with those flowers, but perhaps there are paths invisible to me still."

"It's the individual lives you can't predict," Michelle said, "which makes them more interesting."

She felt Brenda smile against her cheek. "Yes."

"Will I remember all this when I wake up?" Michelle asked.

"No," Brenda said. "You can't. No one who receives this kind of wisdom can live an untroubled life."

Brenda stepped back and gestured toward the river with her head: *Shall we?* They walked hand-in-hand toward the water.

MICHELLE WOKE UP freezing on the bathroom floor, wondering how she got there. She crawled back to the bed, and buried herself under the sheets.

WHEN MICHELLE WENT down to the hostel lobby with her bags on her last day in Hong Kong, only the old woman was there behind the reception desk. "Checking out?" she asked. Michelle nodded yes. This close, Michelle could now read the name on the woman's pin: Shuang. Michelle wondered what her name meant.

Michelle peered closely at the photos on the wall. Shuang noticed her looking and spoke to her in rapid Cantonese, pointing at the framed photos one by one. A photo of Shuang as a child, her face smooth, scar-less. Shuang wearing a school uniform. Shuang with a group of girls having sandwiches in a park. Then the newspaper clippings about the war, the headlines screaming. Shuang pointed at the burn scars on her face and neck, at a spot on her abdomen. Michelle waded through the old woman's foreign words until familiar words jumped out at her like wild animals: "mama", "bayonet".

Shuang walked from behind the counter and now stood next to her. "Philippines!" she said, and there Shuang was in the photo, a teenager, scarred but smiling in front of Manila Bay.

Michelle smiled too. "You lived in the Philippines?"

Shuang gestured with a hand. *Just for a little while.* She pointed at a man in an Army group photo, and touched her chest.

"Husband?" Michelle asked, and laughed when Shuang giggled like a teenage girl.

What followed were photos of a wedding, dinners, family reunions, a tall teenage girl wearing graduation robes, a photo of three chubby babies in matching red strollers. Shuang pointed to her scar again, then gestured toward the photos. "Gets better," she said, looking at her. "Yes?"

She couldn't quite explain it, but Michelle felt gratitude well within her, felt the tears brim in her eyes. She nodded. "It gets better," she said.

THE MISSING

There were only six of them, but several times during their trip in Thailand, Harold would think that they were missing one person. During dinner he would catch himself saying, *Let's wait for*—and then realize that there was no one left to wait for, as he counted his seated friends already digging into grilled fish and steamed rice at the sidewalk stall. *One two three four five six.* Inside Platinum Mall, as they made their way through hordes of fellow tourists buying scarves and cheap shoes, the sudden bursts of Filipino words (*Mahal, Ang ganda o, Tawaran mo pa*) causing both confusion and delight, one of his friends said, "Meet you downstairs at closing time?" and Harold very nearly said, *Okay, but we should tell*—

One two three four five six.

There was no one to tell, but Harold felt the uneasiness nestling in his bones, the same disquiet that invaded him whenever he left his rundown Makati apartment in a rush: *Did I leave the light on? Did I lock the gate properly? Did I unplug the computer?*

Am I forgetting someone?

HE WASN'T SUPPOSED to be on this trip. He already said no back in October, when his friends were still putting together the itinerary, trawling travel blogs and TripAdvisor comments and consequently bugging him online. They were friends he met back in high school. They went on to different courses and universities, and got updates on each other's lives only through social media and the once-in-a-blue-moon dinner or coffee. They still carried with them the clinginess of high school cliques, but now coupled with work schedules and good salaries. *What do you mean, no? You have VLs left, don't you? It won't cost much, Harold, we'll stay at budget hotels. Come on Harold, you've been looking so sad lately. You certainly could use a vacation.*

IN HIS HEAD was a black cloud, a steady rain. He couldn't shake off the inexplicable darkness that had come over him more than a month ago. He couldn't pinpoint the exact date now, but he remembered the exact moment. He just came home, tired after having emerged from payday traffic, happy for purchasing a new book, and sat down in his apartment without turning on the lights. The darkness settled. He couldn't remember the book's title anymore, and wondered why he even bought it. He was twenty-eight, he was alone in the apartment, and the purchase of the book was the high point of his day. Why was he so happy earlier? What was the point of that happiness?

After this payday would be other paydays, where he would come home alone, again, with another meaningless little token. He felt the realization like a wound. *Is this it, then? Is this all?*

He emailed his friends and asked them to book him a flight. They cheered, and Harold thought he should be grateful to have friends like them. He should be a better person. This lifted his spirits for a moment, but the thought made him feel guilty and pushed him to the depths again. A vicious cycle. He closed his eyes on the plane as the speed of takeoff pushed his body against the backrest. He imagined his boss, a jolly old woman of fifty, telling him the usual platitudes. *You're still young.*

You're still young, you're just killing time. You're still young, it will pass.

He was waiting for it to pass. He couldn't wait to be old enough to look back and sneer at his aimless, sourceless sadness, sneer at his young foolishness.

BANGKOK WAS THE last stop in their nine-day trip, after having passed through Vietnam and Cambodia. Their hotel in Thailand was a cheery two-story in an alley off Silom Road, past several massage parlors, restaurants, and a curiously located art gallery.

During their first night there, Harold dreamt that he was making a bed. He positioned the thick mattress on a handwoven mat in the middle of the wooden bed frame, tucked in the white sheets and the checkered brown duvet, fluffed up the pillows.

He was talking about his trip in Hanoi, the
night market that reminded him of Paco, the beautiful
bridesmaid he saw riding a scooter on a major road,
completely made up with a fascinator in her coiffed hair
and green paint on her lids, her yellow dress hiked up to
her thighs. He was amused, he said, by how she looked
more comfortable, more beautiful, than his friends in the
air-conditioned tourist shuttle. In Siem Reap, he said, the
hotels were lined up on either side of the main street, one
after the other, like houses. All because of the Angkor
Wat, he said. It's a recipe for success, if you're a monarch:
create a big structure, jumpstart tourism after it falls into
ruin.

He said he felt humbled as he walked through the
temple, surrounded by bas-relief, by apsara dancers and
their graceful limbs. Here was an empire, long conquered,
long gone, still providing for its people.

After he was done straightening the sheets, he asked,
"How's that side looking?" to the figure on the other side
of the bed, but Harold woke up before he could hear the
answer.

IT WAS DRIZZLING on their last night in Bangkok,
but his friends insisted on walking along the sidewalk to
look at the things on sale. Some tables carried sex toys,
engorged penises like tent poles pushing up the plastic
sheets that the vendors had thrown over them to keep
them dry. "Ping-pong?" said a short man, pushing a piece
of laminated paper to Harold's face. The paper contained a
list of prices. "Pussy?"

"No, thank you," Harold said, as his friends snickered beside him.

They went their separate ways to cover more ground, and Harold found himself walking with his friend, K. "How much?" K asked at a stall selling embroidered wallets. Harold reached up to the pashminas hanging from the stall's roof, touched the golden threads, wondered idly if his sister would like one. K was busy haggling down the price. "Okay!" the vendor suddenly said. It's raining, he said, profit is down, and the customers should have their way.

"That's right," said K, smiling, and chose two wallets in bright pink and green.

K moved on to key chains (the Grand Palace, elephants), and Harold felt again that invasive belief that he had left someone behind and should turn back before it's too late.

There was someone looking at him from the next stall.

Harold felt it as much as he felt K beside him, haggling once again and gesturing with her hands.

The light was coming from behind the stalls, so the customers were all in shadow. The stall was selling souvenir shirts (*Tuktuk as Taxi!*), but the person wasn't looking at the shirts; the person was looking at him.

Harold moved forward to ask a question, but the shadow turned and ran.

Before he could fully understand what was happening, Harold was already running down the sidewalk, colliding into the ping-pong hawkers, the tourists holding umbrellas. "Wait!" he shouted, *I just want to know who you are,* but after a while he forgot why he was running, and stopped. To his right was a tiny mall, two stories brightly lit, the words SUPERMARKET! SPICY TAMARIND! flashing green on the ground floor façade above a blood-red awning.

He heard someone panting behind him and turned. K was bent over on the sidewalk, hands on her knees.

"Harold!" she said. "What the hell?"

"I'm sorry," he said.

"Oh my God. I thought someone snatched your bag. What happened? Why did you run?"

"I don't know," Harold said, and helped K walk back to the stalls.

HE DREAMT ONCE again of making a bed. It was the same bed. White sheets, checkered brown duvet. This time, however, he was aware of a few more details. There was a window showing gray skies, a small pot with a tiny cactus on the white window ledge, soft carpet on the floor. The sheets felt cool in his hand. The bed was inviting in the humid heat.

"Tourism is a funny thing, isn't it?" he said. He talked about Corregidor, which he visited last year—how their tour guide said *Here are the suicide cliffs where soldiers chose to jump to their deaths rather than be taken prisoners* as though she was simply telling them where they could pee.

"Sometimes they don't tell you all the stories," Harold said. Like: *More than a decade ago, in Cambodia, three women held a young mistress down on the ground, and the scorned wife poured two bottles of hydrochloric acid on her face. Who will love you now?*

Someone will always love you. The pain dulls and you become a ruin of yourself, and one day you will guide people into your halls, your avenues and your temples, and they will talk of your tragedy, and they will talk of your grandeur.

"Someone will always love you," Harold said, out loud, and the realization came.

"I'm making this bed for you, aren't I?" he asked the person on the other side of the bed, before the alarm clock woke him up.

HOURS BEFORE THEIR flight back to Manila, Harold made his announcement. He was going to stay behind. Just a couple more days, just to clear his head. His friends were worried. They asked if there was something wrong. Is there a problem at work? Did he want them to call someone back home?

"No," he said. He just wanted to be alone.

K, more brazen than the others, drew him aside and asked him if he had been having suicidal thoughts.

Harold laughed. "Why in the world would you think that?"

"You've been withdrawn lately. And what was the deal last night? Why did you suddenly run?"

Harold didn't know what to say.

"Are you heartbroken?" K asked.

"I'm not even dating anyone, K."

K fell silent then, looking at him, sizing him up.

"You have enough money?" she asked. "You've talked to the hotel about the extension? You've told the airline?"

"Yes, *Mother.*"

"I swear to God, Harold, if you kill yourself, I will fly back here and slash your throat."

HAROLD THOUGHT ABOUT K's question. *Are you suicidal?* Through the black cloud and the rain, not once had he thought about it. He didn't want to die. He couldn't imagine death.

If he were dead he wouldn't know why he was sad, and he wanted to know.

Are you heartbroken?

He had never been in a relationship, but there were close calls, the harrowing almosts. People who picked him out from the crowd and later decided, *No, not for me.*

It felt like this, he thought. Was this it? Sadness compounded from all those past almosts?

ON HIS FIRST morning alone in Bangkok, Harold bought breakfast and lunch at the food stalls. Pad Thai and rice noodle rolls, Pathong Ko with condensed milk and pandan leaf custard dip, mango and sticky rice. For merienda he bought two chopped sausages and an iced tea, and stayed in his room, staring at the ceiling. At night he took the BTS to Siam Paragon and walked its gleaming hallways, hoping movement and window-shopping would cheer him up.

Already he was thinking that choosing to stay had been a mistake.

He wasn't hungry the next day, so he stayed in bed until five p.m., still wearing his clothes from last night, clicking through the channels like a dying man. When it started to get dark, he put on new clothes and his pair of sneakers.

He walked down Silom Road, past the sidewalk stalls, past McDonald's and Happy Lemon, past the escalator going up to the Sala Daeng BTS station. The restaurants and shops on the sidewalk beyond the escalator were closed, save for one café. The café had bare wooden tables, white flowers as centerpieces, soft yellow light. A tiny bell tinkled when Harold opened the door. He chose a table in the corner, behind a plant box acting as divider, away from everybody else.

"There you are," Harold heard someone say.

The man was his age. He was wearing a black jacket over a blue shirt, jeans, sneakers. He sat across from Harold at the same time the server came with a glass teapot.

"Khob kun krub," he said before the server left. From his accent, Harold could tell he was not Thai. Maybe also Filipino, like him.

"Look," the man said, indicating the teapot. Inside was a flowering white tea, now starting to bloom. It looked like an exploding sun.

"Who are you?" Harold asked.

He was watching the tea steep. "Look," he said again, and Harold saw that the flowering tea had become a ball again.

"Are you a ghost?" Harold asked.

"A ghost." He sounded amused. "Maybe. A future ghost."

"I don't understand."

"I'm afraid you'll meet me soon, Harold. I don't know what my role will be. Maybe a close friend. Maybe a colleague. Maybe—"

Harold felt bold. He remembered his recurring dream, a room with a bed.

"Maybe a lover," Harold said.

He smiled then. He had a nice smile, Harold thought.

The tea began blooming again. After a moment, Harold picked up the glass teapot and poured them some tea. Harold took a sip, and asked, "Why did you say you're afraid?"

"What?"

"You said you're afraid I'll meet you soon."

He was silent for a while. The tea tasted like peaches.

"You've been sad lately."

"Yes."

"Do you know why, Harold?"

Harold shook his head.

"You will find me, but you will lose me."

"What?"

"I don't know how, or how long from the day we meet. Months? Years? A decade? But you will lose me, eventually."

"You don't know that."

"Do you know why you are sad?" he asked. "Because you are already mourning me."

The flowering tea was a ball again, Harold noticed. "So you're saying the future is set in stone?" he said.

"One particular future is. The future you strayed into. But now that you know what's waiting for us in the end, do you think it will still be worth it, saying hello to me on the day we meet?"

"People love all the time," Harold said, "without knowing what the future will bring."

"I know," he said. "They're the lucky ones."

Harold felt something cold creep up his leg, and he jerked, waking up in his hotel room, in bed, with the TV still on. He was still wearing his clothes from last night.

"K?"

"Harold! You're still alive. Well done. What are you doing now?"

"Just watching TV."

"You wanted to stay in Bangkok just to watch TV?"

"Do you know that there is a theory saying that the past, present, and future happens all at once? So the past is still with us, and the future is already here. Our concept of time is causally and serially based because it's the only way we can comprehend time and the only way we can function."

"You wanted to stay in Bangkok just to bore me with this?"

"But what do you think?"

"You're saying the future is set in stone," K said.

"But maybe there are multiple universes," Harold said, "and they are all here, all at once, and you can cross from one to the next, depending on your decisions and actions. Maybe there are several futures, and you get to choose."

"I'm sure our course in Metaphysics 101 has already covered this, Harold."

Harold sighed. "I'm sorry, K."

"Are you all right?"

"I guess I'm just feeling lonely."

"Then come *home.*"

HE STARED AT the screen of his laptop for several minutes, and finally booked his return flight. He shut down his laptop, took a quick shower, and put on new clothes. He was going out for a walk.

He was thinking of buying some squid balls when it began to rain. Hard. The nearest shelter he found was a mall. Harold ran. There were already several people there, and he squeezed in, securing his spot beside a couple hugging each other and watching the rain come down in sheets. The words SUPERMARKET! SPICY TAMARIND! flashed over their heads.

The people left, one by one, as the rain lessened in intensity. Harold saw him when the couple stepped out of the awning under a large black umbrella. He was wearing a black jacket over a blue shirt. He bounced lightly on his toes, as though getting ready to run.

Now that you know what's waiting for us in the end, do you think it will still be worth it, saying hello to me on the day we meet?

Harold stared at him, and looked away.

There are many ways to lose someone. A fire. An accident. Cancer. A morning when everything is clear, and you realize you've changed your mind.

Harold remembered the steady rain in his head, the days when he couldn't eat or sleep, and wondered what could possibly cause that, wondered if he could survive it.

Should I say hello? He felt the future standing beside him beneath this awning in Bangkok, one thousand four hundred miles from home, and imagined a life with an ending that could bring him joy.

Harold looked to the sky. The rain would be over soon.

The rain would be over soon, Harold, he thought, and took a deep breath.

A PRAYER TO THE MANY-EYED MOTHER

Alejandra and Ava stared at her while they sipped their raspberry iced tea. Alejandra had won twenty dollars from one of the slot machines earlier and used it to buy fries for the table. No one was eating them, and they now sat limp and greasy in the wire-mesh basket.

"So," Ava said, "you're here to ask for a green card?"

One of the craps tables erupted. Someone had won. Ruby sipped her coffee and said nothing.

"I didn't mean to offend," Ava said. "It just seems like such a high price to pay."

"We did say Grand Café, right?" Ruby said, craning her neck. It was midnight, and there were only a handful of patrons inside the restaurant.

"Are you really related to her?" Alejandra asked. She lowered her voice. "You know—*the witch?*"

"She's a distant cousin," Ruby said. "I met her when I was a little girl. I remember visiting her at home in the province every summer until my mother decided we're not to talk to her anymore."

"And she found you on Instagram?" Ava asked.

"I didn't even know she was in Vegas until she commented on one of my photos."

"What does her house look like? Do you remember?" Alejandra asked.

"No." Ruby turned to her. "Why exactly are you here, Alex?"

"Alejandra," Alejandra said.

"Sure," Ruby said.

Luciana arrived at that point, sliding into their booth with a drink in hand, talking a mile a minute: "—so there I was with three vouchers worth eleven dollars each, and I put them all in this machine with Cleopatra's face on it and I got the major bonus of 100 dollars and I kept betting and this lightning sound came and I got eight bonus spins and I saw Cleopatra's eyes filling up the screen and—"

"*You're* the witch?" Alejandra said.

Luciana lost her smile and stopped talking.

Alejandra was flustered. "I'm sorry, I was just—"

"Were you expecting someone who smelled like dead rat?" Luciana, who was wearing a black cocktail dress and large earrings that sparkled in the restaurant's dim light, took a clumsy swig of her whisky and coke, sloshing some of the drink onto her hand. She did not smell like dead rat. She smelled like sweet Pink Apple perfume mixed with Black Velvet Whisky.

Luciana turned to Ruby and smiled. "Honey!" she said.

"Hi, Ate Lucy," Ruby said. "You're not drunk, are you?"

Luciana took one of the fries from the basket. She held it in her fist for a second, and opened her hand to reveal a small yellow snake. Alejandra and Ava shrieked, causing some of the patrons turn their heads.

"I'm drunk," Luciana said, letting the snake wrap its body around her wrist like a bracelet, "but you don't need me anyway. At least not after I give you the instructions. You'll be doing most of the work." She waved her other hand over the snake, and it fell to the table, a limp fry again. "How did Ruby find you two?"

"Reddit," Ruby said.

"*No,*" Luciana said, and slammed a hand on the table in delight. "That's amazing!"

Alejandra had the look of someone beginning to regret their decision.

Luciana downed another swig of her cocktail. "Okay," she said. "You all have Filipino blood, correct?"

"I was born here," Ava said, "but both of my parents are Filipino."

"My mother is Bulakeña and my father is from Cavite," Alejandra said. "They migrated here before I was born."

"Thank you for the family history lesson," Ruby muttered.

"What?" Alejandra said.

"Is Filipino blood necessary for this to work?" Ava asked.

Luciana began to giggle. "No, darling. I was just curious."

"Oh."

"If you don't mind me asking," Alejandra said, "how did you end up in Vegas?"

"I married an American, dear," Luciana said. "He was 20 years my senior. Then he got very, very sick, then he died, and now I spend my nights getting plastered in front of slot machines." She stared off into the distance, finishing her drink. After a silent beat, she turned to Ruby. "Marriage. That's something to consider, you know. To get a green card? Instead of this?"

"If the Many-Eyed Mother can grant any wish," Alejandra said, "why didn't you wish for your husband to be cured?"

Luciana sighed. "You may be too young to understand, but some people, after much pain and suffering, they just decide they're done with life. They've seen enough, they've done enough. They'd rather rest."

"But oblivion is not rest," Alejandra said.

Ava shifted in her seat. "Maybe you should stop asking all these personal questions."

"You loved him, didn't you?" Alejandra pressed, with the treacly eagerness of a noontime variety show host.

Luciana and Ava stared at Alejandra with a look of confused revulsion. Ruby rolled her eyes.

"We don't need to talk about why we're doing this, right?" Ava said. "I mean, because I don't want to talk about it."

"Oh, definitely," Luciana said. "I don't care. That's between you and the Many-Eyed Mother."

Alejandra swallowed audibly.

"She sees all," Luciana said. "Do you really want to go through with this?"

They looked at each other. Luciana reached a hand into the wire-mesh basket, picked up a handful of fries, and began to eat them.

"Last chance to back out," she said. "I won't be mad."

"I'm not backing out," Ava said.

"Yeah," Alejandra said. "We're going through with this."

Luciana nodded, looking impressed. "And you?"

"I'm in, Ate."

"Okay." Luciana wiped her fingers on the table napkin and took out a folded piece of paper from her purse. Ruby reached out for it, but Luciana snatched it back at the last minute.

"At least one of you needs to go through with this," she said, "or endless harm will come to you." She held their gaze. "And that endless harm will come from me. You have no idea what I'm capable of."

"Okay," Ruby said.

"I'm not kidding, Ruby. I can turn a fry into a snake, and I can do the same to your intestines."

Ruby felt a jolt of terror. "I said okay."

"Okay." Luciana handed her the paper, and snapped her fingers to call a server. "Hello? Can somebody give me a menu, please? I'm dying over here."

They unfolded the paper in the parking lot while standing next to Ava's car.

HELLO! DO YOU REALLY WANT TO DO THIS?
DO YOU REALLY REALLY WANT TO DO THIS?

ARE YOU SURE THAT YOU REALLY REALLY REALLY
WANT TO DO THIS?

"For fuck's sake," Ava mumbled under her breath.

"We are sure, right?" Alejandra asked.

Below the message was a residential address on West Tropicana Avenue.

YOU'LL GET FURTHER INSTRUCTIONS ONCE YOU GET
TO THE HOUSE. THE DOOR COMBINATION IS 3467.
DRIVE SAFE!

"I like your cousin," Alejandra said as they settled in the car. Ruby sat in the back. "She's quite a character."

They pulled out of the casino parking lot.

"Can I drop by my house for a sec?" Ava asked. "We're near West Tropicana so it won't be too much of a detour."

"It's your car," Ruby said.

Alejandra glanced at Ruby through the rearview mirror.

"What do you do back home, Ruby?"

"Are we really doing this?" Ruby said. "This isn't a road trip."

"All right, jeez," Alejandra said. "I'm just making conversation."

Ava took the 215, tapping her fingers on the steering wheel.

"I'm a copywriter," Ruby said after a few minutes.

"That's cool."

"My relatives who left the Philippines worked blue-collar jobs," Ruby said. "I don't know what the hell I was thinking, expecting to get a cushy office job here. Tita Chona worked as a domestic worker in Hong Kong for many years before moving here to work at a casino. My own father worked for five years in Taiwan. Do you know what his favorite job-related story is? Being driven around Taipei in a Volvo, except that the Volvo belonged to his boss and he and his co-workers were being driven to the boss's house to earn some extra cash by cleaning up his living room for Chinese New Year."

"Your relatives are very brave to leave home to provide for their family," Alejandra said, and Ruby suppressed a groan. "Is that why you're planning to leave home?"

Ruby closed her eyes. The reasons passed behind her eyelids like the pictures on a zoetrope: standing inside the MRT with her breasts squashed against another passenger, running after a bus and elbowing a woman away in order to get a seat, losing a day's pay after the government closed several roads without prior notice so visiting state officials wouldn't experience Manila's infamous traffic, the Philippine peso plunging to 52 against the dollar, her inability to save enough money despite her many side gigs, the sudden increase of her electric bill, the daily reports of death related to the drug war, alighting a jeep in Divisoria only to find her backpack slashed and her wallet stolen, eating a Mini-Stop hotdog while waiting for the Friday traffic to die down and feeling so lonely and weary and miserable she wished the ground would just open up and swallow her, standing in the sunlight outside the Parañaque LTO for three hours only to be told that new driver's licenses would not be available today, thank you, please just come back tomorrow, and growing angrier every day, the anger growing as large as the guilt because what was she complaining about, really, you earn a salary and eat three times a day, what's wrong with you, you should be marching on the street and fighting this drug war and the government corruption that you say you hate so much instead of finding a way to leave the country—

Ruby tried to sift through these reasons and formulate an answer, but couldn't.

About 15 minutes later, she glanced out the window and saw a large brass sign that said *Spanish Trail*. Alejandra whistled as they drove up a driveway and stopped in front of a yellow-lit mansion the color of the desert.

"You live here, Ava?" Alejandra said. "What do your folks do?"

"They're surgeons."

"Do they need a dishwasher?" Ruby said, only half-joking.

"I won't be long," Ava said, unbuckling. After a moment, she seemed to reconsider. "Do you want to step inside for a minute?"

They stood at the entrance to the family den. An episode of *Sneaky Pete* played with the sound on mute on the 120-inch TV. A young girl who resembled Ava sat on a fluffy area rug, earphones plugged in her ears, typing on her laptop. Without looking up, she said, "Mom's going to kill you."

"*You're* still up," Ava said. To Alejandra and Ruby, she said, "That's my sister, Rita." And as if to defend herself, added, "My parents are out on a call, and they said it's okay if I went out tonight."

"Rita Hayworth and Ava Gardner?" Ruby said. "Cute."

"I have schoolwork," Rita said, still not looking up from her laptop screen. "Are you out because of schoolwork, Ava?"

"I just need to get something," Ava said, and ran across the floor and up a staircase they couldn't see. Alejandra and Ruby remained standing by the entrance, hands in their pockets. Rita continued typing.

Ava came back a minute later. "Okay, let's go."

"It's amazing," Alejandra said as they drove away from Spanish Trail. "Our parents coming here to give us a better life."

Ruby laughed. "A better life," she said. "I wonder what kind of life I've led so far, then."

"I would love to go to the Philippines, you know," Alejandra said. "Find out more about my roots."

"Why are you here, Alejandra?" Ruby said.

"Guys," Ava said, "I thought we agreed not to—"

"It's fine," Alejandra said. She glanced at Ruby. "I'm writing this novel set in Manila—"

"Oh, perfect," Ruby said. "That's just perfect."

"What?"

"You have the Philippine flag symbol next to your Twitter handle, don't you?" Ruby said.

"What?"

"I bet you went by 'Alex' until you got bit by the Pinoy Pride bug and thought the Anglicized version of your name is somehow less pure. You should take it a step further. You should start calling yourself Awit or Kawayan or Ilog or—"

Silence.

"I feel like you're mocking me," Alejandra said.

"Publishers would love you," Ruby said. "You speak unaccented English and have exotic stories to tell. Filipino but not too Filipino. You know? We have writers back home who would never receive the kind of exposure you will receive—and you haven't even been to Manila! Thank you in advance for the representation. Tell me again how brave my relatives are. Tell me again how magical the Philippines is."

They drove down West Tropicana Avenue in uneasy silence. The address was in a quiet neighborhood jutting out into the desert. Every house was the same shade of ochre and had the same potted succulent on the front porch. Ruby always found the silence of US suburbs eerie. Her Tita Chona lived in a neighborhood like this, and Ruby had never seen anyone out on the street past six p.m., had never even heard the hum of conversation spill from behind the smart-locked doors.

Ava decided to park one street away. They walked to the house and stood shoulder to shoulder on the front porch. Ruby held the piece of paper from Ate Lucy in front of her, right hand hovering over the touchscreen.

"I'm on your side, okay?" Alejandra suddenly said, making Ruby jump. "Representation in whatever form is—"

Ruby sighed and keyed in the combination. The door opened with a whir, and they stepped into a living room lit only by a small lamp. There was a piece of paper stuck to the lamp. Ruby hit her knee against the couch as she rushed over to read:

YOU MADE IT!
GOOD JOB!
NOW OPEN THE DOOR TO YOUR LEFT.

They all turned their heads to look at the door.

"Okay," Ruby said, rubbing her knee.

"Is this Ate Lucy's house?" Ava asked, picking up a framed photograph from the side table. It was a photo of Luciana and her blond husband at Red Rock Canyon, his sunburnt face nearly the same shade of burgundy as the mountains behind them.

"Why would she make us go to her house?" Alejandra said.

Ruby, who didn't know the answers, walked over to the door and opened it.

Inside the room was a woman, bound and gagged. She was sitting on the floor. She began struggling against the duct tape wound around her wrists and legs when the door opened, and screaming as best as she possibly could from behind the ball of cloth shoved inside her mouth.

Ruby slammed the door shut.

"What the fuck," Alejandra said.

"There was a," Ava said. "There was a piece of paper on the floor."

Ruby opened the door again. The woman, tired from screaming earlier, now sobbed, her eyeliner making her tears visible as they rolled down her face. She had a large wound on the crown of her head, the blood coating her hair. She was wearing a black shirt, jeans. One foot bare and covered in tiny cuts, the other clad in a black sneaker.

The floor was covered with plastic. Next to the door was a plastic jug with a post-it note that said CHLOROFORM! (LIKE IN THE MOVIES!) and a folded piece of paper.

I TOOK THE LIBERTY OF SECURING THE SACRIFICE. NOW ALL YOU NEED TO DO IS GOUGE OUT HER EYES FOR THE MANY-EYED MOTHER.

"Jesus," Alejandra said.

NOW DON'T BLAME ME: I DID ASK YOU MANY MANY TIMES IF YOU REALLY WANTED TO GO THROUGH WITH THIS. NO SUCH THING AS A FREE LUNCH AND SO ON. NO CONSEQUENCES HERE SAVE FOR YOUR WISH— BUT ONLY IF YOU FINISH THE RITUAL.

p.s. SPEAKING OF FREE, FEEL FREE TO GET FOOD & SODA FROM THE FRIDGE. RITUAL IS HUNGRY WORK! JUST DON'T FREAK OUT WHEN YOU SEE THE OTHER STUFF IN THERE.

p.p.s. PLS DON'T GET THE REMAINING CAN OF DIET SUNKIST, I'M TRYING TO SAVE THAT FOR TOMORROW. SMITH'S ALWAYS RUNS OUT OF DIET SUNKIST. I HATE THAT.

Ruby walked to the kitchen and opened the fridge. Next to the butter and eggs and leftover Spam and cream cheese were jars of eyeballs suspended in cloudy liquid, bloody nerves and veins trailing behind them like tadpole tails. One jar was empty. NEW EYES HERE! the note said. Ruby took out the empty jar and walked back to the living room.

"I'm going to be sick," Alejandra said.

"Please don't," Ruby said.

The woman's sobs now had the shape of words. She was pleading with them.

Ruby closed the door, handed the jar to Alejandra, and sank into the couch. Alejandra and Ava joined her. They sat for several minutes in stunned silence until Ava said, "Now what?"

"Guys," Alejandra said, still hugging the empty jar to her chest, "I don't think I can do this."

"You figure your novel's not worth all this trouble?" Ruby said. Alejandra placed the jar on the coffee table and covered her face with her hands.

"My mother would know how to properly gouge out eyes," Ava said. "She wouldn't even cry, or overthink what she's doing. She's like granite."

"She's a surgeon," Ruby said, feeling compelled to state the obvious.

"I would love to be like her," Ava said. "To be like granite. Instead of—" She took a deep breath. "Well, what did we expect anyway? It's not like Ate Lucy would ask us to plant flowers."

Alejandra lowered her hands from her face. "We can't do this if the woman in there is tied up like that. We need to lie her flat on the floor."

"We need to knock her out," Ava said. "There's chloroform in the room."

"She's going to scream once we remove the gag, though," Alejandra said.

Ruby grabbed a clean dishrag and pocketed a pair of scissors from the kitchen. They went back to the room. The woman started struggling and pleading again, until she looked past Ruby.

Ruby glanced over her shoulder and saw Ava standing by the door with a gun.

"Holy—" Alejandra said.

"Is that what you took from your house?" Ruby said.

"Hurry up," Ava said, pointing the barrel at the woman, who had gone as still as a statue. "Look, lady," Ava said, licking her lips. "Um. Don't scream. Okay? Or I will shoot."

"Not in the head though," Alejandra said, "because we need—maybe in the neck?"

"I can't believe we're doing this," Ruby said. She felt her stomach drop. "I think we should just let her go."

"What?" Ava said. "No. No. We're doing this."

"I can talk to my cousin. We can work it out." Ruby sighed. "This is *crazy*."

The woman looked up at Ruby with hope in her eyes. Ruby stepped forward and saw the woman's bound hands behind her back. She stopped cold. There was a ragged cut in the duct tape, and the woman was holding a small, dull-looking knife. How long did it take for her to reach into her pocket or her socks to get that knife, to cut herself free?

Ava trained the gun on her. "If you untie her, Ruby, I will shoot you."

"Okay," Ruby said. The woman stared at her, holding her gaze, not blinking. "I'm just—I'm just removing her gag."

She grabbed the end of the gag with her thumb and forefinger, and pulled out the spit-drenched rag from the woman's mouth. The woman coughed, began to retch.

"Oh, please don't throw up," Alejandra mumbled.

"Give the dishrag to Alejandra," Ava said. Ruby did as she was told.

"What's," Ruby said, as Alejandra drenched the dishrag with chloroform. "What's your name?"

"Don't do that," Ava said. "We don't need to hear that."

The woman lifted her head and stared at Ava with blank eyes.

"I was there when the first of my daughters began to see," she said.

They stopped moving.

"What?" Ava said.

"I see everything," the woman said. "I see the light. I see the void. What I see, you can never survive. I borrow your eyes to see a different life, to experience not knowing. To escape, even through your darkest days. And you have a lot of dark days, don't you, Ava?"

"How did you know my name?" Ava said.

"I understand the need to just fade away, Ava. To not hurt anymore. To not hurt anyone."

The gun in Ava's hands began to tremble.

The woman shook her head, and when her hair fell away from her face, her eyes looked at Ava and the gun in horror. "My name is Pam," she said, sobbing again.

"Please. I work at Orleans. Please. Please just let me go. I won't tell anyone."

"What the hell?" Ruby said.

"Out of the way," Alejandra said, holding the rag now drenched with chloroform.

Pam lunged at Ava, her hands now free. They all fell back in surprise. Ava crashed into Alejandra and Ruby dropped to the floor, leaving the door wide-open for Pam to hop through. "Here!" Ruby shouted, and took out the scissors from her pocket to cut the duct tape around Pam's feet. A moment later, she was running.

Pam ran to the kitchen and began to slide open the glass door that led to Luciana's small backyard and the dark, shapeless desert. Ava pointed the gun at her and pulled the trigger. Pam shrieked and dropped to her haunches. The bullet hit the coffee machine on the counter, making glass fly in all directions.

Pam slid the glass door open and ran into the desert, screaming for help. Ava ran after her.

"Wait!" Ruby shouted. She felt her shoes sink into sand, felt grass whipping against her ankles. She touched her jeans pocket and swore. Her phone was not there. She couldn't see anything, save for the gun in Ava's hand, glinting in the distance as she ran. "Ava! Just let her go!"

A gunshot. And another.

Something slammed into Ruby. She screamed. But it was just Alejandra, gripping her shoulders, peering at her with wide eyes.

"We need to go back," Alejandra said.

"No, Ava is—"

"I can't run anymore," Alejandra said. "Okay? We need to go back."

They limped back to the house. While standing in the living room waiting for her thoughts to coalesce, Ruby found her purse with her phone in it. There was a message from Luciana.

YOU DID IT! (OR AT LEAST ONE OF YOU DID.)
THE MANY-EYED MOTHER IS PLEASED.

Ruby turned to Alejandra and saw her holding up her phone. She had received the same message.

"Pam from Orleans," Ruby said. "Jesus Christ."

They walked with heavy steps out of the house, into a street, a world, that felt fundamentally different. They tried to look for Ava's car but couldn't find it.

"She probably already left," Alejandra said.

Alejandra glanced at her screen while Ruby booked an Uber. "Why would you want to go back there?" she demanded after seeing the destination.

But Ruby wanted to know if Ava was safe.

Rita, her laptop resting on one arm, earphones still plugged in her ears, answered the door.

"Yeah?"

"Hi," Ruby said. "Is Ava home?"

Rita frowned. "Who?"

"We were here with her earlier," Alejandra said.

"We just wanted to check if she made it home safe," Ruby said.

"I think you got the wrong house," Rita said, and began to close the door.

Ruby put her arms up. "Wait, wait. Ava's your sister, right?"

"Who the hell's Ava?" Rita said. "I don't have a sister."

"But—"

Rita glanced over her shoulder. "Mom?" she called. "Dad?"

A middle-aged woman in scrubs holding a large mug of coffee appeared next to Rita. *She's like granite,* Ruby remembered Ava saying.

"They're looking for some lady named Ava," Rita said, and skipped away from the door.

"I'm sorry," the woman said. "There's no Ava here."

"That's impossible, we were just here with her a few hours ago—"

"Never met them before, Mom," Rita said from inside the house.

The woman smiled. "Please leave."

"But—"

"Please leave before I call the police."

They ran down the street and kept running until they reached the Spanish Trail brass sign. In the Uber, Alejandra covered her face with her hand and began to sob.

"Is your friend all right?" the driver asked. Ruby leaned her forehead against the window and closed her eyes.

WHEN SHE GOT back to Tita Chona's house, Ruby called the airline, packed her bags, and announced that she would be leaving the next day.

"Already?" Tita Chona said. "But I haven't even taken you to Trader Joe's yet!"

Ruby mostly slept during the 15-hour flight. She dreamt of a shelf full of jars, each jar with an eye staring at her.

The plane landed in Terminal 1. Her SIM reconnected to the local network, and the texts came one after the other: her parents asking her if she finally got a job offer, her sister asking if she bought the jacket and the shoes she liked, her cousins asking if she could take them to Duty Free and did you get any chocolates?

A man approached her at the entrance, offering to help her with her bags and get her a taxi.

"Balikbayan?" the man asked.

Ruby was tired. "No, sorry," she said, putting on her sunglasses and switching to the American accent she had perfected while working at a call center during her college years. "My family's picking me up. I'm just here for vacation. Excuse me."

Undeterred, the man switched to English, giving her tips on where she could go "for a good time". "I have a van your family can rent," the man said. "You should go to Baguio. The weather is cooler there. You're used to cool weather in America, correct?"

"We'll take Uber," Ruby said, and walked away, rolling her bags behind her.

"But Baguio's too far for an Uber!" the man called after her. He turned to another person behind him. "Hello! Balikbayan?"

Ruby entered a nearby eatery to get away from the stifling heat. She looked up from the sauce-splattered laminated menu and stared at the television mounted on the wall. It was tuned to the news. An old woman in Tondo faced the camera, crying. Her sixteen-year-old son was shot on the street by three masked men on motorcycles. Ruby wondered what that mother would give to get her son back and end this suffering, what she would do to not be powerless, to not be dismissed, to not be here at all.

THE SEVENTH

She arrived at the house on a perfect morning—
gentle sunlight, light breeze, the pleasant smell of coming
rain. She knew, somehow, that it wouldn't be a destructive
downpour, just a wispy shower to water the flowers. She
knocked on the back gate, and the caretaker's wrinkled
face appeared to greet her through the peep hole. "Oh," the
old man said. "It's you. Did you have a nice walk?"

She smiled and ignored the old man's strange remark.
She got here straight out of the bus, what walk was the old
man talking about? Inside the kitchen, she saw a tray with
two plates by the sink. One of the plates contained half
an omelette and a slice of bread, the other had traces of
ketchup and a spoonful or two of rice. Leftovers.

"Is there someone else here?" She wondered who else
could be here. Her siblings? Her cousins? The caretaker
looked confused, mystified.

"What do you mean?" the old man asked.

She pointed at the tray. "You have a guest?" She
didn't mean to sound obnoxious. Her grandmother had

that tone with the help, but then the caretaker was not supposed to have guests in the house.

The caretaker took a moment to answer. She noticed him looking at her shoes, the hardened mud like brush strokes, the dried leaves stuck to the soles. Instinctively, she lifted one foot to check what he found so interesting there.

"Are you all right, Julia?" he said.

She frowned. "I am," she said, slowly, putting her foot down again. "Why?"

"Those are our plates," the old man said. "From earlier today? Remember? We had breakfast."

She shook her head. "I just got here."

"You've been here seven days."

Silence, then she started to laugh. "No. I just got here. I literally just got off the bus fifteen minutes ago."

"No." The caretaker looked perplexed, and a little frightened.

She sighed. His father was right. The old man was getting confused. Just like her grandmother before she died. "It's okay. You can go home now. I'll just call you when I need anything."

"You've been here seven days," the caretaker said.

She was starting to feel irritated. "No," she said.

"You have. You were up there and you were studying. Then after breakfast you went out for a walk."

She counted to ten in her head. Took a deep breath. "I'll just call if I need anything," she said, and steered him out through the kitchen door.

IT WAS A beautiful house with a flourishing back garden and expensive furniture. Her family wasn't rich, but her grandmother was, so the house with the flat screen TV and the hot shower and central air and a soft couch that didn't vomit its cotton stuffing was where she threw her birthday parties, where she took her boyfriends, where she stayed for nights on end when she needed some time alone.

The bedroom upstairs was neat and smelled of disinfectant spray—a tangy, lemony odor—and certainly didn't look or smell like a room where someone had slept for a week. She wondered how the caretaker was doing, if he was still thinking, *If that wasn't you, then who have I been talking to for seven days?*

She shivered and stood by the window. The window overlooked the garden, with its white chairs and white table. Beneath the table was something she had never seen or noticed before: an opening of a water well, covered with a slab of plywood. Was it new? She had been coming to this house for years and had never seen that well before.

She started unpacking, placing her clothes in the closet, placing the books and her notepad on the study table. She was studying for the engineering board exams, and passing the board would mean she would be able to follow one of her uncles to Qatar, an impossible place where water was more expensive than gasoline. *They'd probably give everything for that well outside*, she thought.

Often, she would wonder why she even tried so hard. Either she would be in a freak accident or she would live until the ripe old age of 90. Either she would be injured or she would forget all of it, in the end, like her grandmother who died at eighty-eight with her memory jumbled up. Confused, unwanted, moved from one son's house to another. Whatever brightness her grandmother had Julia was never able to witness, which was a tragedy in itself. Lucky number 88. *I still have sixty-eight years of lucidity left*, Julia thought, sitting at her desk with her structure formulas and her design methods. Sixty-eight years didn't feel like such a long time.

SHE WAS WRONG about the rain. When it fell that night, it fell hard, hammering on the table and the chairs and the flowers, the wind whistling through the gaps in the windows and the doors, through the floorboards, the cold banisters. She tossed and turned in her sleep, hearing something moaning in pain, hearing a clear voice saying, *First a warm bath, then you will be left hanging here until your bones are dislocated.* In her dreams she was sure the moans were coming from the covered well.

SHE WOKE UP later that night to the sound of banging coming from the back of the house. Someone was knocking on the kitchen door. An urgent, insistent knock, like the knock of someone who was being pursued.

But the only person standing outside was a woman in a crisp shirt and a pair of jeans, waiting with her hands folded by her chest, like an orator or an opera singer. Julia had never seen her before.

The woman was searching Julia's face for something, and when she didn't see it she dropped her hands and her shoulders, put on a worried expression. Julia noticed the flashlight sticking out of the pocket of the woman's jeans. "I'm so sorry to bother you," she said, "but I think a kitten of ours fell into your well? I've been hearing it for hours, but I'm not sure if it's real or just my imagination."

Oh, how terrible, Julia thought, but then she remembered the sounds from a few hours ago, the moans cutting through the rain. That wasn't a kitten.

"Can we," the woman said, pointing with her flashlight to the well under the table, "can we check? I'm sorry. I'm too scared to check on my own."

Julia would be terrified, but not at that moment. The terror would come later, much later, after she had returned the woman's smile, after she had said "Yes, of course", after she had walked through the garden, after they had pushed the table aside, after she had knelt by the well's weather-beaten plywood covering and pushed it off with the heels of her palms.

First there was the smell. Putrid, overwhelming, a smell that reminded her of hospitals and animal cages, of powerlessness and shame. It was the smell of feces, urine, vomit. The woman swung her flashlight's beam to the well and Julia absorbed the scene in bits and pieces: a tattered shirt, a stained piece of fabric fashioned like a hammock, a scalp covered in scabs, a hand reaching up toward the opening, toward her, toward light and Julia screamed and scrambled across the ground, scraping the palm of her hands, hitting her forehead on the kitchen door. The woman's shadow fell across her like an eclipse. Julia ran deeper into the house.

"SHOULD WE GO through this again, Julia?" the woman said. The woman's name was Sylvia, a name that floated out of the ether. Why does she know the woman's name? Julia, who had locked herself up in the bedroom, could hear herself huffing like a dog. She couldn't breathe. She crumpled to the floor and hugged her knees, covered her mouth with both hands to stop herself from screaming. She had never before felt terror like this, a terror that seized her insides and made her shiver as though she were pushed into a vat of ice.

"Julia," Sylvia said. The knob turned and Julia screamed.

"Julia," she said again. "You know what you saw."

There was a woman in the well, and the woman was wearing her face. She looked the way Julia would have looked if her teeth were kicked in, if her hair and fingernails were torn out, if she were dehydrated and starved and tortured for hours. The woman in the well was unrecognizable as Julia, but Julia recognized her with one glance.

"You go into the well and your new version that appears in this house goes through the same stages of fear and denial," Sylvia said on the other side of the door. "Over and over. You are the seventh version now. What does this tell us, Julia? That perfection does not require memory?"

Sylvia had a key. The door opened and Julia rushed at her, shoving her aside. Julia ran down the stairs and tripped on something—a leg chair, the edge of the carpet, her shoelaces. She fell hard. She sobbed with her face against the floor and couldn't get up.

"You have legs now," Sylvia said. "Use them and sit at the table with me."

Why was she doing what the woman told her? She should be running now. She should be attacking her. She should be—

"It will come to you," Sylvia said, disappearing into the kitchen. She came back a few minutes later carrying a tray. On it was a cheese sandwich, a bowl of cookies, and iced tea. Sylvia placed the tray in front of her.

"During your last hour in the well, you always start singing," Sylvia said. "It's a simple tune, and it's always the same tune, but it's in a language I don't recognize. Maybe one day you will be able to tell me what you're singing about."

"I don't understand," Julia said, crying. Weren't she just studying a few hours ago, figuring out the logistics of living abroad, listening to the rain fall as she fell asleep?

"What did you notice in the sixth version?" Sylvia said. "Hm? What did you notice when you saw the Julia in the well?"

I am not a version, Julia thought but couldn't say. *There is no Julia in the well because I am the only Julia.*

Sylvia said, "What was she missing?"

Julia didn't know what Sylvia was talking about. Then she was reminded again of the smell that hit her when she uncovered the well, the emotions she associated with it. Shame. Powerlessness. Disgust. Why was she reminded of hospitals? Why did the caretaker stare at her feet, why that brilliant smile, that pride in his voice when he asked, *Did you have a nice walk?*

"She didn't have any legs," Julia said, and the world tilted slowly, like a leaf on a placid lake.

"It was late at night," Sylvia began, and continued to tell the story in the bored tone of someone who had been telling the same story over and over and over, "and it was dark and you were hurrying down the street from work and you didn't see the opening in the ground, the drain grate without the grate, and you fell and you injured your legs. The fall was only ten feet. You would have been able to shake that off, but there was debris at the bottom, sharp glass, rusty rotten things, and you struck them, and you weren't found for hours." Sylvia sighed, shrugged. "The doctors had to amputate from the knees down."

"No," Julia whispered to herself, touching her legs, but the world was still tilting to fit this new perspective, and the world was telling her Yes.

"You wanted your suffering to mean something," Sylvia said. "It always means something in stories, doesn't it? Your own Catholic parents had faith that an individual's suffering can cleanse the world and rid the rest of us of further pain. There are people who refuse medical treatment because they believe suffering has a purpose. If your suffering could bring your legs back, if it could make you better, then the pain would be worth it. Right? That's what you told her, and she said she could do that, she could show you."

"Her?" Julia said.

"Or him," Sylvia said. "Or it. The one you found at the bottom of the drain, the one who held your hand after you got tired of screaming for help."

Julia felt fear like an electric shock.

"I don't remember any of this," she said.

"That's what all the other versions say," Sylvia said.

"I don't know who you are."

"But you know my name, right? I was there at the hospital, and you told me this story. I was there because my entire family died in a bus crash. What else was there left to believe? But I believed you." Sylvia glanced at the clock on the wall. "Hour before midnight. Sooner or later you're going to climb back into the well. I can't wait to meet your eighth version. You came back with both legs on the seventh day. Maybe on the eighth you would be calmer." She smiled as though this were a long-standing joke between them.

"I am not going in there," Julia said.

"I know," Sylvia said. She grabbed the cheese sandwich from her plate and took a bite. "You always say that, and yet before midnight you'd have lowered yourself in the hammock, begging me to cover the well."

"What happens in there?" Julia asked, at the same time parsing together a path out of this house, down the road, her legs taking her to the bus station and away.

"Suffering that has meaning," Sylvia said. She was quiet for a moment. "But you never tell me the specifics. Once, you told me there is someone waiting at the bottom of the well."

"I want to get out of here," Julia said, and found herself crying again.

"You always say that, but you never do," Sylvia said. "Look, I'm not stopping you. Get up and leave if you want."

Julia wanted to, but her legs felt leaden. Sylvia wore a triumphant smile. See? that smile said.

"Remember your grandmother telling your family that she didn't want to end up like her mother?" Sylvia said. "And her mother before her, and her mother before her. It runs in your family, that awful disease. She said she'd rather die than inflict that kind of burden on her children. Remember how that broke your heart? If only she were still alive. If only we could put her in the well."

Julia thought of her grandmother sitting at the table and touching her arm to say, "Who bought this? This food looks expensive." The food came from their kitchen and was cooked by her mother, but in the ruins of her grandmother's mind she believed she was in a restaurant, enjoying an expensive meal with a bunch of strangers who looked vaguely familiar. Who bought this? And Julia, who knew there was no need or time to reason or explain, said, "I did, Lola. I bought this for you."

There was no need or time to reason or explain.

"What version are you, Sylvia?" Julia asked, changing her tone, making her sound sweeter.

Sylvia wiped crumbs from the corner of her lips. It took a while for her to reply. She looked ashamed. And hungry. "I have never been in the well."

"But you wanted to go?"

There was no hesitation. "Of course."

Julia nodded. "Why don't you go this time, Sylvia?" she said. "I will wait for your new version. I'm sure she will need someone here to explain things to her."

Sylvia's eyes filled with tears. "You will do this for me?" she said.

SYLVIA CHATTERED ON as they walked to the well. The midnight air was cold, and Julia could hear nothing but Sylvia's voice, as though everyone else in town had died. "I wonder, does your consciousness move from the old version to the new, like water, or does one, the superior one, just obliterate the other?"

"Aren't you afraid of the pain?" Julia asked. She remembered again the lacerations on the arms of the person in the well, the blood in her mouth.

"I've been through worse," Sylvia said. "Imagine, a driver who fell asleep at the wheel, just three seconds out of his many hours on the expressway, and he obliterates my entire family. Imagine that. Imagine the senselessness of that. At least in the well, my pain would amount to something."

The well was empty. A new hammock was strung up in the middle of it, white and pure. Beneath this white fabric was darkness that went on and on and on.

Sylvia took off her shoes. She sat on the edge of the mouth of the well, and with Julia's hands in hers, slowly lowered herself to place her bare feet on the fabric.

"Do you think I would also sing?" Sylvia asked, her face white as the moon inside the well. "Do you think you'd be able to understand the words?"

Before Julia could think of an answer Sylvia glanced back and suddenly tightened her grip on Julia's hands. "Wait," she said. "Wait. No. Get me out of here. Get me out of here! Get me out of here!"

She pulled Sylvia up without a word. Sylvia's grip relaxed, and Julia opened her hands and let go.

Sylvia did not scream, or did not have the chance to. Julia waited for several minutes for the sound of water, for the sound of impact, but it did not come.

She replaced the cover and turned to run back into the house, to get her clothes, to gather her books, to leave this place. She looked up at the last minute and saw the curtain twitch behind her bedroom window. She threw herself at the back gate, for a horrible second thinking it was locked, but the gate yielded, and she burst out of the garden onto the dark road, running as fast and as far as her legs could take her.

AYANI

Her name was carved into the rocks. Eva couldn't understand how she could have missed them, the deep grooves that spelled—

"Ayani."

Now named, she had to be given a want. What does Ayani want?

"Something to drink," Eva said. Of course. Like the Aesir, Khal Bhairav, the prophet Elijah, or the Redeemer's blood offered at the graves of the dead.

She went back to the tree where she carved a tally of her days. Ninety tallies total. Beneath the tree, the crate with Antonia's red wine. Eva had prayed to God, to the Virgin Mary, dear St. Anthony please come around something is lost and cannot be found. "They can't find me," Eva said, raising the bottle of wine. Perhaps Ayani could answer her prayer, now that everyone else had fallen silent.

The prayer was not answered. Eva woke up and she was still on the island, Patrick's single-engine plane leaving a black line across the forest. The wine was not enough.

What does Ayani want?

"Fish," Eva said. Patrick and Antonia brought enough food to last a few weeks, but Ayani did not want dried fruit, or cereal, or black tea, or meat—Eva knew this in her heart. "I will get you fish, Ayani," she said, and she walked into the ocean, grabbing fish with her bare hands, screaming in pain as their fins cut deep gashes in her palms. She cried as she arranged the fish on the sand, in a pattern most pleasing to Ayani (Eva knew this in her heart), as she fell to her knees and raised her bloodied hands. "Please help me," she said. "I beg you."

The prayer was not answered. Eva took the fish and ate them raw as penance.

What does Ayani want?

"Worship," Eva said, and so she hiked to the plane where Patrick and Antonia were still strapped to their seats. They were naked now and hairless, as Ayani had intended, their skin purple and black, torsos like a deflated balloon. Eva unstrapped them and pulled them down the plane, and the maggots fell from them like rose petals. Eva's chest filled with joy. "Praise be to Ayani!" she cried.

That night she built several small fires in the forest, and danced with Patrick and Antonia in Ayani's honor. *Ayani, Protectress! Ayani, my goddess!* They raised their arms, clapped their hands, twirled on one foot. Eva did not dig a fire pit (as Ayani had intended), and the fire leapt to the surrounding trees. Fire touched Patrick and Antonia, and they ran deeper into the forest, screaming, *Praise be to Ayani!* The fire raged for days, and Eva danced until her palms were chafed raw from clapping, until her feet bled. When the rescue planes came, she saw Ayani in the light. "I am not worthy!" she shouted, blinded by Ayani's beauty, as she was bundled up, as needles were stuck in her arms.

What does Ayani want? Eva thought, airborne.

She understood completely now.

"Acceptance," she said, staring at the sky outside the window.

"What was that, miss?" the doctor said, and Eva smiled, imagining the plummet, the return to Ayani's bosom. Maggots would fall from the doctor's hollow chest like rose petals. Praise be to Ayani.

Queen Midnight

"They say its eyelids have gone down another meter," Abi said, her voice echoing in the stairwell. "It's just a matter of time. Maybe in three years, it'll finally close its eyes and stop giving us nightmares."

"Are you looking at Bakunawatch again?" Mimi asked, the balloon squeaking in her hands. Abi raised her phone. The screen showed the monster's face, eyes like a pair of bloody tumors protruding above sharp, pointed teeth the size of skyscrapers.

Paula frowned at them both. "What a stupid name," she said. "It doesn't even look like a sea serpent." Scientists had likened it to the giant Grenadier fish, a deep-sea fish with large mouth and eyes, except that this one was truly gigantic, with the tip of its head resting on what used to be Alesund in Norway and its tail brushing what used to be Krasnoyarsk in Russia, a body length of more than 4,000 kilometers. Some fiction writer, in an attempt to reference local mythology, called the creature "Bakunawa" on social media. Her post was shared more than eighty thousand times, and now the name still stuck, five years after the Surfacing. She also coined the term "Surfacing", to describe the day the creature began to appear from the depths of the ocean. A girl's got to do what a girl's got to do, Paula thought. Some turn to naming the unnamable; others join a sad, undermanned, underfunded, wish-granting nonprofit organization, pretending the world is still sane.

They were sitting on the stairs of the apartment building where the Child of the Month lived. It used to be an affluent building, but after the Surfacing it had fallen into disrepair, like most other places. The stairwell was dark, made darker by the gray clouds outside, threatening rain. The elevators and corridors smelled like dog pee, and Paula had earlier stepped on what could either be wet mud or feces.

The balloon in Mimi's hands exploded, the sound as surprising and deafening as a blast. "Jesus!" Paula said.

"Sorry," Mimi said, looking distraught.

"Maybe we should give up on the balloons," Abi said. "We're not making any headway, and we only have thirty minutes left."

"The boy asked for balloons," Paula said, reaching into the box next to her for the hand balloon pump. "Let's give it fifteen more minutes."

Abi sighed. "I'll go fix Mimi's eye makeup."

They managed to make four balloons—one shaped like a poodle, one shaped like a cat, one shaped like a monkey, and one shaped like a sort-of horse with one ear and three legs. "It's the effort that counts," Abi said, indignant, when Paula stared at it five seconds too long.

"Not really, Abi," Paula said. "But sure, whatever you say."

"I play better than I make balloons."

"And thank God for that."

They didn't want to smell like the elevators, so they took the stairs. The apartment was only two flights up.

"If the mother requested for media coverage," Mimi said, "do you think HQ would have given us a PA?"

"Do you need a hand with your case?" Paula asked.

"No," Mimi said. "Just wondering out loud if the organization still cared about us."

The floor where the boy's apartment unit was located looked and felt abandoned. Every door they passed was locked, with poorly spelled signs announcing that the previous residents had moved out, and to contact the building supervisor for rent inquiries or to get the forwarding details. There were boxes on the corridors filled with toys, bedsheets, clothes, books, bric-a-brac, all covered with a thick film of dust. Abi peeked into one box and found kitchen appliances: a toaster, a microwave, a blender. Mimi found a laptop under several pillows.

"Do you think this still works?" she asked.

"Don't touch anything," Paula said.

Abi stood next to Mimi and pinched one of the pillows with her thumb and forefinger. "This is goose down!" she exclaimed.

"What did I say about not touching anything?"

"I'm coming back for those pillows," Abi said.

Paula knocked on the door and readied her smile. The door was answered by a woman with smeared lipstick and a large gold-orange stain on her white blouse. "Good morning," the woman said. Paula's smile faltered a little.

"Mrs. De Vera?"

"That's me," Mrs. De Vera said. "Well." She stood in the doorway and stared at them for an awkward minute. "I didn't expect to see a group of young ladies. I thought only old biddies volunteer for this kind of thing."

"I'm twenty-one," Mimi said, who was often mistaken for a high school student, making her touchy about her age.

"Good for you," Mrs. De Vera said. She looked up at the balloon animals and Abi's sort-of horse bobbing against each other. "How sweet. You brought balloons."

"Andrew asked for balloons, didn't he?" Paula said as they entered. "You know our tagline, 'You dare to dream, we dare to make your dreams—'"

"Where *is* Andrew?" Abi asked, looking around the two-bedroom apartment. There were traces of child in the living room: rubber shoes and balled up socks, basketball jerseys, a stack of discs on top of a black game console, a child-sized violin. On their left was a curtain running the length of the room. The curtain was thin and made of cloth, making Paula think of a hospital curtain. That side of the room was dark so they couldn't see any shadows or silhouettes, though they could hear a faint sound of blowing air.

An automatic room deodorizer and humidifier sat in the middle of the coffee table, but on top of the fragrant fumes, Paula could detect a rotten odor, the smell of decaying seafood.

"Let's get a drink first," Mrs. De Vera said, herding them away from the curtain. "Just us ladies."

"Paula," Mimi said, leaning close so Mrs. De Vera wouldn't hear, "is it just me or does this room smell like fish?"

The kitchen was immaculate, a stark contrast to the large stain on Mrs. De Vera's top. She opened one of the cupboards and took out a bottle of whiskey and three glasses. She placed these on the kitchen table and opened the refrigerator to take out a liter of soda and a half-empty ice tray.

On the table were several magazines and paperback books about deep-sea creatures. One slim volume opened to a poem:

The Sea Monster as Goddess

Blessed be The Sunken Mother, now Risen, now free.
Truly—
Only in the depths can one find true Beauty
That even blind eyes can see.
The earth splits open, the ocean peels
off its sun-soaked mask
And lets Queen Midnight bask in Her glory.
"Come to me," She whispers, "come to me,
All the dying, all the drowning,
The tired, the hungry—
Come to me—
And I will swallow you whole."

"We will just take the soda, please," Paula said, slightly rattled, and closed the book.

"All right," Mrs. De Vera said, handing them glasses, and mixed herself a drink that was more whiskey than soda.

"It must be hard," Mimi said, clutching her own glass to her chest, "to take care of Andrew all on your own."

Mrs. De Vera did not acknowledge this. Instead she said, "Where were you during the Surfacing?" but didn't give them a chance to answer. She continued: "I was at work. There was a terrible earthquake. I thought, 'This is it. The Big One.' Remember when they kept talking about that? That we're due a big earthquake and have to be prepared for the worst? Drills every quarter, but where was the metro-wide Gigantic Monster Drill when you needed it?"

She laughed weakly. She placed her elbow on the table and cupped her cheek. Her face was turning red from the alcohol. "I didn't even know anything about the ocean. Do you know that 97 percent of all habitable living space on earth is in the deep sea? And that there's a region in the deep ocean called the Midnight Zone, where sunlight doesn't penetrate at all? I've also only learned recently that there's a thing called 'abyssal gigantism'—ocean creatures that live in shallower waters become giants when they live in the deep. Scientists think it could be adaptation to scarce resources or ocean pressure, but they still don't know exactly why it happens."

Paula, Abi, and Mimi glanced at each other. None of them had the heart to tell Mrs. De Vera that yes, they knew all this, they had talked about it ad nauseam and picked apart all the existing theories on Reddit and Facebook, they had read all the Wikipedia entries.

Governments rained bombs on the monster as it continued its ascent, unperturbed, cracking open Eurasia, creating tsunamis that sank islands and countries. During those early days, there were several reports of people falling ill because of the monster, especially the people still living in relative proximity to the site of the Surfacing. Lung inflammation, seizures, vomiting, internal bleeding, skin damage—all symptoms of acute radiation syndrome. But no one came forward with definitive proof.

For two years after the monster completed its ascent, it gradually opened its eyes, and now it appeared to be closing them again, a multi-year blink. That was it. That was all.

Mrs. De Vera finished her drink and led them back to the living room. Paula took out a small tripod and a video camera from her bag and began to set up, Mimi and Abi standing close and hovering over her in their nervousness. When they looked up, Mrs. De Vera was standing right in front of the lens, looking as if she were on the verge of punching their throats.

"What are you doing?" she said.

"This is for documentation, Mrs. De Vera."

"Didn't I say no cameras?" She went to the coffee table, picked up a plastic bin full of toys and upended it, letting the contents fall to the floor. She marched back to them with the empty container in her hands and said, "Give me your phones, all of your gadgets."

Paula was indignant. "Mrs. De Vera!"

"You'll get them back!" The woman was genuinely shouting now, a vein throbbing in her temple, the skin on her chest turning red. "Give me your phones now!"

Mimi turned to Paula with frightened eyes, as if to say, *We are going to die here, aren't we?*

Paula, who had not moved a muscle, said, "Mrs. De Vera, you are scaring the performers."

Mrs. De Vera stared back at her, blinked, took a deep breath. The throbbing vein disappeared, the redness on her chest drained away.

"You know what TMAO means?" Mrs. De Vera asked in a small voice.

Paula, surprised, could only say, "What?"

"Trimethylamine N-oxide," she replied. "It's what makes fish smell like fish." She placed the bin on the floor. "Giant Grenadier has high concentrations of it. Makes it smelly. Makes my house smelly."

She grabbed one end of the curtain and spoke as she pulled it aside. "I've always wondered what that thing is planning to do after it surfaced. It just floats there. It moves so slowly. What the hell does it even want?"

The curtain revealed a plastic tent, the kind of tent they used to isolate patients with Ebola.

"Now I think I know," Mrs. De Vera said.

Inside the tent, they could see two pale legs wrapped around a thin, white blanket. From the chest up all they could see was black: black, shiny scales, huge black eyes, a slit of a mouth. The legs twitched every three seconds. All over the bedsheets was a large rust-colored stain. As Paula tried to make sense of the scene before her, she thought of the stain on Mrs. De Vera's blouse, the stain she at first thought was whiskey. The legs twitched, and the stain on the bed grew wider. The stain was coming from the scales.

"It's turning us into its likeness," Mrs. De Vera said.

None of them screamed, although Paula could feel herself trembling.

"We were told he had cancer," she managed to say.

"And you don't consider this cancer?" Mrs. De Vera said, her voice rising again. "When I filled out your wish-granting form a week ago he only had scales on his chest." A few moments later, when they failed to move, she made an impatient gesture with her hands. "Well?" she said. "What the hell are you waiting for?"

They had swallowed their screams and now the screams were propelling them, making them move like automatons. They stared at the floor, pretending the tent and the boy in the tent did not exist. Paula fixed the stands and placed the sheet music titled *Passacaglia in G minor on a Theme by George Frideric Handel for violin and viola (Halvorsen, Johan)*. Abi and Mimi lifted their bows and began to play.

Paula didn't know much about classical music, but she was instantly transported, away from this room, away from this planet with a monster in stasis. After the initial high, however, she began thinking that the Passacaglia sounded mournful, like a funeral dirge, and she wished they had played something else instead. Some piece not by a Norwegian composer who was not only dead but whose country was dead as well, blown to smithereens by a monster head rising from the sea.

Every now and then Paula would glance at the tent and see Andrew's legs twitching, twitching.

Five and a half minutes into the piece, while Paula watched Abi and Mimi sway with the music and the movements, a pained scream came from inside the tent.

Andrew was attempting to stand up.

Mimi, who was playing the violin, paused for a moment. "Don't stop playing!" Mrs. De Vera pleaded. But that slit of a mouth opening to show wound-pink flesh, that pained scream like a cross between a small child and a dog pinned by a car, was making it difficult to do anything else.

Andrew stood on unsteady feet. Now his whole body twitched, spraying rust-colored drops. Mrs. De Vera shouted her son's name. Andrew tripped over the tangled sheets and hit the wall of the tent, bringing it down with him as he fell. Mrs. De Vera, tears streaming down her face, knelt in front of her son and placed her hands over the plastic. To Paula's horror, she saw Mrs. De Vera tighten the plastic over Andrew's head. The fish-head. The plastic fogging up with breath, the mouth gaping wide. "It's okay," she said. "It's okay, it's okay."

Mimi picked up the stand and her case with surprising ease and ran out of the apartment. Paula and Abi followed close behind. One of the balloons got caught in Abi's viola case and exploded, making Paula shriek. They could hear a steady, dull thump against plastic, a gush of viscous liquid, and Mrs. De Vera's voice saying, "It's okay, baby, it's okay, it's okay", the sounds following them down the dark stairwell.

THEY BURST OUT of the lobby doors and kept running for several blocks until Mimi yelped and sat down on the sidewalk, massaging a cramp. Now they sat next to each other on the steps of what used to be an office building, the steel handles of its glass doors wrapped with a rusted chain, threaded through with a padlock the size of a child's face. CLOSED UNTIL FURTHER NOTICE, a sign taped on the doors said. Below it, someone had written in an angry scrawl, *Behold, Behemoth, which I made as I made you,* followed by *There go the ships, and Leviathan, which you formed to play in it.*

They sat for ten minutes, not saying anything, just letting the silence settle, letting their muscles rest. Finally, Abi said, "The tent came from the government, didn't it?"

"What?" Paula said.

"It has to have come from somewhere," Abi said. "It's not like you can buy one of those at S&R."

"I think you could," Mimi said. "They sell camping tents."

"Whatever," Abi said. "Someone supplied that tent to her. The government knows about this."

Paula sighed. "Save it for the Reddit thread, Abi."

"Do you think the disease is caused by an airborne virus?" Abi said.

Paula and Mimi didn't respond.

"The boy destroyed the tent when we were there," Abi continued. "Mrs. De Vera had a stain on her blouse. And she shook our hands. Served us drinks." She leaned forward. "If I end up like that—"

"Abi," Paula said, touching her temple. "Stop. Just stop talking for a minute."

Paula started thinking of her mother. Her mother who had four children, whose husband left her shortly before Paula's youngest sister was born. She and her siblings had stayed with their mother after the separation, fiercely loyal, fiercely protective. How strange it must have been for her mother, to look around her house one day and realize that she had inadvertently given birth to her own allies, her own lifelong companions. *The monster, the goddess.* Is that what it was doing? A singular creature creating children in its likeness, creating companions to conquer the loneliness?

"Maybe it's just time to step aside," Mimi said.

"What do you mean?" Abi asked.

"For us," Mimi said. "Humans. Maybe it's time for us to step aside. Maybe our time has come. What good have we ever done for the planet anyway?"

It would be a relief for the planet, Paula thought, to have millennia of only stillness and small, quiet movements. For once.

"Well," Abi said. "As long as we don't suffer, I guess."

"Do you think Andrew is suffering?" Mimi asked.

They didn't have an answer for that.

"I will miss music," Mimi said. "And food. And the beach. I used to really like the beach, but now I can't even stand staring at a large body of water."

Another quiet minute passed. Black clouds were gathering overhead. It would rain soon, and Paula didn't have an umbrella. She had to contact HQ and request for transportation. Once they returned to their shared apartment, Abi had to do her laundry, Mimi had to clean the refrigerator. And Paula had to prepare dinner and write a full report about what happened.

Even now, even here, they had to do these things as though they were the most important things, as though they still had an infinite number of days before them.

"Abi?" Mimi said. "Can you play Stravinsky's Elegy?"

Abi yawned and glanced at her. "Sure," she said, breathing deeply as she stood up. "Why not."

Abi placed her chin on her instrument. Her bow slid across the strings, making a sound like that of an animal dying, or about to awaken.

AFTER THE CRASH

Diane eventually died from her injuries a week after the crash, and so Julius took his other sister Bernadette from the hospital to their parents' house to make arrangements for the funeral. Julius didn't drive, this time; he hired a driver to pick them up and drop them off. He sat with Bernadette in the backseat and tried not to stare as she picked at the scabs on the knuckles of her fingers.

"You are lucky," the driver said. The driver was a friend of one of their uncles, and knew about the accident. He said they were lucky to have walked away from that car with only minor injuries.

Their relatives said the same thing at the wake, as though the driver had handed out flyers with instructions on what to say to them. "Yes," he would hear Bernadette say every now and then, as they gazed at the closed casket, the gleaming box looking large and foreign in the middle of their mother's living room. "Lucky."

He was thirty, Bernadette was twenty-nine. Diane, the baby, dead at twenty. *The curse of life is you never fully realize how fortunate you are,* Julius thought. When he was Diane's age, he would look in the mirror, grab his flab, hate himself for being out of shape. If he could travel back in time, he would scream at his 20-year-old self: *So what if you were out of shape? You want to hear about hating yourself? At least you still had parents. At least you haven't crashed your car with your siblings in it. At least you haven't killed your sister.*

They both decided to stay in the house, using up their vacation leaves from work, keeping busy by cleaning the rooms, going through the artifacts of their childhoods, like archaeologists going through layers of soil. "Remember this?" Julius would say as he held up an old PE uniform, a participation ribbon from kindergarten, a framed photo of Diane and Bernadette dancing during Family Day.

After their parents died, Diane had continued to live in the house, watering their mother's plants, running their father's small store in the wet market. They saw her everywhere they turned. They bumped into her boxes of secondhand books, her piles of moth-eaten clothes, her discarded CDs, her—

"What's this?" Julius said, holding up a pair of dolls, made of twigs and tied together with jute string. Though the dolls were faceless, Julius could tell it was a man and a woman, the woman wearing a dress, the man tall and thin, like a telephone pole. The dolls, covered with dust balls, were wedged deep in a closet full of old bed sheets and pillowcases.

Bernadette glanced briefly at him and said, "The engkanto."

"What?"

"The engkanto," she said, folding Diane's clothes. "You remember. Father's engkanto. He talked about them."

"I don't remember."

"He told us about them." Bernadette sounded impatient. "Give them here. I'll keep them in my room."

They bought food from the nearby wet market, where they used to play as children, weaving in and out of the stalls like flies. What used to be as familiar as the backs of their hands now seemed novel to their high-rise-dwelling, grocery-shopping eyes. "I think that old lady's weighing scale is dishonest," Bernadette complained once. "I think she uses her fingers to weigh down the potatoes." They picked this issue apart for hours, reveling in the complaint, in the smallness and luxury of it.

One day Bernadette set off for the market alone, leaving him to rest with his headache. He had frequent headaches now, ever since the accident, the pain like a shovel, gouging out ditches in his brain. He was sitting with his eyes closed on the porch, thinking fresh air would help, when he heard someone call from outside the gate.

"Excuse me?" a woman's voice said, issuing forth between the hanging baskets of his mother's unruly portulaca. "Excuse me?"

Go away, Julius thought, and stood up with a groan. He walked to the gate, shading his eyes from the sun.

Outside were a man and a woman, the woman a head shorter than Julius. She had long black hair and wide black eyes. She looked friendly, her face open and pleasant. The man, who had a thin, ragged face, looked scared and tired.

His left shoulder was slightly raised, as though bracing himself for a blow.

Both, Julius saw, had thick bracelets made from jute string.

"Yes?"

"We would like to speak with you," the woman said. She had her hands wrapped around the bars of the gate. "We owe you a favor."

"Sorry, who are you?"

"We were in the other car," the woman said.

Julius felt a sharp pain in his skull, the shovel digging, digging, digging.

"We heard about your sister," the woman said. "We are sorry. We owe you a favor."

"There was no other car," Julius said, and hurried back inside the house.

"MAYBE THEY'RE THE engkanto," Bernadette said, during dinner.

Julius paused halfway through a bite of soy-sauce-drenched potato. They were having Bernadette's beef steak, which Julius always found too salty. "That's quite a leap," he said.

Bernadette shrugged. "Father said when he was young, a very old tree in the backyard would turn into a man and a woman and talk to him. One day they asked him if he would like to owe them a favor. Father said the woman was very pretty. He couldn't take his eyes off her. But he said no. He thought if he said yes and asked for something incredible—like a million pesos, or a cure for his brother's polio—the engkanto would ask for something incredible in return. Like flood the town, or burn down the piggery. He said the tree moved out of the backyard, and he never spoke to them again."

"The tree moved out of the backyard?"

Bernadette didn't return his amused smile.

"Father told you that?" Julius said.

"He told us that. You never listen. That's your problem, you never listen."

Julius finished eating his salty potato, feeling that he was being reprimanded for something larger than this conversation.

They fell silent. Julius was tempted to ask, *Was there another car?* But of course not. He knew that.

It had been raining, it was slippery. He avoided what he thought was a tree in the middle of the road, but it was just the rain, playing tricks on him. The car flipped and flipped again and smashed against the side of a building. Diane was strapped in the passenger seat, the side that received the most damage. There was no other car.

"If they were the engkanto," Julius said, "why would they be driving a car?"

Bernadette sighed. Julius could tell she was getting tired of talking. "I don't know. Maybe you're in a postmodern story."

Julius scoffed. "That's not what postmodern means."

She looked at him as if to say, *If you're so smart, why did you crash the car?*

"Maybe I just heard them wrong," he said.

THERE WAS ALWAYS someone dead in the news. "There was a guy who pretended to be delivering a package," Bernadette said, paraphrasing the news anchor, "so this woman let him in. He then dragged her to the kitchen and raped her and hit her with a hammer."

"Jesus."

"It happened just two towns over. Terrible, isn't it."

Bernadette sounded more curious than horrified. Sometimes Julius wondered if Bernadette watched news about heinous crimes out of a desperate need for schadenfreude. *My sister is dead, but at least she didn't die like that.*

"The poor woman," Julius said.

THAT NIGHT, HE dreamt of a man and a woman turning into dolls made of twigs. The dolls walked out onto the road, dragging their jute strings, and turned into a tree on a traffic island. The tree appeared in the center of his windshield, like a dark spot in his vision.

AFTER THE FUNERAL, the days seemed to bleed into one another, making Julius feel as if he were enduring one endless day without rest. This fevered state of mind was heightened when the man and the woman appeared outside the gate again that afternoon, while Bernadette was sleeping, the woman saying, "Excuse me? Excuse me?"

"What?" Julius said, his anger coming loud and quick like a thunderclap. "What the hell do you want?"

"A favor for you, sir," the woman said. "A boon."

And like a thunderclap, his anger disappeared in an instant. "There was no other car," Julius said, almost pleading. *There was no other car because there was only me, me, me.*

To his surprise, the man turned to the woman and said, in a soft voice, "I told you he said 'car'."

The woman looked confused. "Car?"

"Isn't that what you said?" Julius replied.

"We said we were on the other *lane*," said the woman. "We were on the other lane, and you swerved to avoid us. That happens sometimes. I'm so sorry."

"You were *walking* on the other lane?"

"We didn't say we were walking," she said.

Julius could suddenly feel the heavy weight of the humid air. "All right. What are your names again?"

The man and the woman looked at each other. "Our true names are a bit hard to pronounce," the woman said.

"What is this?" Julius said. "Is this a joke? Do you think this is funny?"

"No," the woman said. "Not at all."

"That's it," Julius said. "I'm done talking to you."

She reached a hand through the bars of the gate. "But don't you want to claim your favor?"

"Why are you so hell-bent on giving me this goddamn favor?" Julius said, angry again. "What will it even achieve?"

But even as he said it, he already knew. What he would give to remove the abyss in his chest. What he would give to go back in time and tell Diane, *Yes, you're right, it might be safer to drive you home when the rain is over.*

"Can you bring my sister back?" he asked.

She pulled his hand back. "I'm sorry," she said. "Our powers have limitations."

"Well," Julius said, stepping back inside the house, "there you go, then."

THAT EVENING, WHILE Julius was washing the dishes, Bernadette poked her head in the kitchen and asked, "Are you having the LPG replaced?"

"What?" Julius could hardly hear her over the sound of running water.

"The LPG? Did you order a replacement?" And then Bernadette was screaming, her scream abruptly cut by the unmistakable sound of a slap.

Julius ran out of the kitchen and found Bernadette in the living room, her mouth covered by a man's hand, a man's arm wrapped around her torso, the man standing behind her, gripping her so tightly, patches of her cheeks had turned white from the lack of circulation.

"Please," Julius said, the shock and fear paralyzing him. Just a few weeks ago, Diane lay in a coffin on the spot where they now stood.

"Shut up!" the man said. "Make another sound and I'll bash her head in."

Bernadette struggled, her slippers slapping on the floor, as the man dragged her to a bedroom. Bernadette's room. Julius's head was filling up with static, the buzzing of bees, the buzzing of words disappearing, as all his faculties failed him in his terror.

The man froze.

In the yawning darkness of the room, Julius watched a shadow solidify into a head, a chest, a hand now grabbing the man's neck, making him loosen his grip on his captive.

Bernadette shook the man's arms off and fell to the floor outside her bedroom window, coughing.

"How did you get in here?" Julius said, as the man with the jute string bracelet stepped into the light of the living room. He was followed by the woman, who gagged the man and tied his hands behind his back, using a pair of pantyhose. She did it all without a word. The intruder had gone as limp as grass in high wind, his eyes wide and searching.

"Are those my pantyhose?" Bernadette said, indignant.

Julius helped her sit on the sofa. "How did you get in here?" he asked again.

"This man has been observing your house for days," the woman said. "Now would you like to claim your favor?"

"Oh, so you're—" Bernadette stopped talking for a moment. "You knew my father."

The woman said nothing.

"This can't be the favor," Bernadette said. "What a waste! I could drag him to the police station myself, and gladly, too. I could kick him in the kidneys."

"What would you want, then?" the woman asked.

Julius wanted to be kind. "They can't bring Diane back," he said, placing a hand on his sister's trembling shoulder.

Nobody spoke for a moment. Julius saw that the intruder, kneeling on the floor, had peed himself.

"Well, what's the use, then?" Bernadette said, brushing Julius's hand off. "Why did you even come here?" She stood up, rubbed her face with her hands. "I'm going to bed." She walked to her bedroom and locked the door.

Julius sank into the sofa.

"If we could bring her back, we would," the woman said. "Please believe us."

"I swerved to avoid you?" Julius said.

"Yes," she said. "You have no one to blame but us."

He had no one to blame but them. It was not his fault. And yet—

And yet.

He lowered his head into his hands and cried.

They stared at him, expectant, waiting.

"The boon, sir," the woman said in a small voice.

After a few minutes, Julius wiped his eyes on his shirt sleeve.

"All right, then," he said. "Just get him out of here. And clean that mess he made."

"And the boon is considered fulfilled?" the woman asked, breathless with relief.

Her companion lifted the intruder and placed him over his shoulders, easily, as if he were a bag of dry leaves.

"Sure," Julius said, standing up to return to the dishes. "Whatever."

BERNADETTE DIDN'T BRING it up the next morning, and so Julius didn't say anything. As the days passed, what happened that night started to feel more and more like a dream. He waited for news about the man's incarceration, for police officers to knock on their door, to get their statements. He wondered if the man and woman with the jute string bracelets even brought him to a police station. Or did they just pull out his veins, turn his skin into bark, make plants grow through his orifices?

In Bernadette's room, his father's twig dolls sprouted tiny, bell-like lavender flowers, their delicate green stems snaking around the dolls' arms. Julius and Bernadette saw this, but didn't have the energy to talk about it.

THEY VISITED DIANE'S grave at the end of that week. They were returning to the city the next day. Back to their jobs, back to their parentless, sisterless lives. On the way there, they started talking about what to do about the house and the store—should they sell? Should they keep the house? Who would look after the properties?—but they soon got tired and fell into a thick, uneasy silence.

There were lavender flowers growing out of the soil around Diane's headstone, the blossoms bending, caressing her name.

"Aren't those the same flowers we saw on the dolls?" Julius asked.

"I don't know." Bernadette sat on the grass, taking out the candle from its plastic wrapping. "I don't know much about flowers."

Julius, looking at the flowers, was hit by a sudden memory. "Remember what we were talking about last year?" Their first Christmas without their parents, sitting around the TV set in the living room, kicking each other's feet like small children. "That I would give Diane away on her wedding day? And then you said, 'What is this giving away business? What are you, used clothes?' You said all three of us should walk down the aisle, with our own bouquets."

Bernadette snorted. "She wanted to meet a guy whose name starts with D," she said, "so they could have an invitation with interlocked Ds on the cover." She was smiling as she said this, then her smile withered, hardened into a frown, as she put the candle in a brass candleholder. The candleholder was too large.

Julius stared at the back of his sister's head, his throat filling up with a weary sadness. When Diane was born, he had stood next to her crib, smiling wide for their father's camera. *This would be your life, Diane. And this would be your death.*

When his father met the engkanto, he should have said, *I wish my son would never be born.*

Julius reached out a hand to touch the lavender blooms, stroking them the way he used to stroke Diane's hair when they were little, on the nights she couldn't sleep.

I'm so sorry, Diane, he thought.

"I'm so sorry, Bernie," Julius said.

"For what?" Bernadette said. She looked at him, and he saw her eyes soften. "Will you help me?"

Julius sat on the grass next to his sister and felt the wind pick up, making the blooms dance, tiny lavender hands waving goodbye.

THE IMPOSSIBLE PLACE

Anton held Eric's hand as he lay bleeding after he was wounded by Belshazzar. It was not the creature's name, but Anton had to give it a name, and it was the name that came to him, bubbling up from his deep fount of Bible verses and shame. He who was weighed and was found wanting.

Belshazzar was eight feet tall, smelling like pus and clad in black, claws as sharp as knives, and it lived in that impossible, sprawling space behind the red door, in the house Anton's family had just moved into. As Anton applied more pressure on Eric's wound, he imagined an alternate timeline where he did not open the red door, where he just took the dusty turbo broiler his mother wanted him to keep in that room, left it in a corner, and went back to his comic book. But the red door opened on a feast—gleaming oak table covered with flowers, wine bottles, fruits, thick cuts of meat—and, entranced, he walked in. Anton did not see the writing on the wall: the dried blood filling the cracks on the marble floor like grout, the dark doorway on the other side of the table that led to many rooms. Eight hundred and thirteen rooms, as Eric had noted.

"A hundred more than the Palace of Versailles," Anton had said.

"It's amazing that you know that," Eric said, which Anton treasured as he would a flicker of light in a dark room.

(When Anton shared this piece of trivia years before in the all-boys Catholic school he attended, someone at the back shouted "Gay!" And Anton replied, in effect, that he *was* gay, but surely people of various sexual orientations have interest in the fucking Palace of fucking Versailles. Then the boy beat him up. Same old same old.)

Eric got lost in the house two days before Anton, through another red door. Between the time he entered the door and the time he lay bleeding stretched two hundred and three days. Two hundred and one days for Anton, then.

All those days of hiding and running and crying, of trying to find the exit and hoping and giving up and trying again. All those days of swiping food from the "Feast Room" that for some reason never ran out of food. The food there tasted like ash, but boys lost in an impossible place can't be choosers, can they.

It was Anton's mother who found them outside the red door. How did they get out? It must have been Eric's blood, which covered them like floodwater. Was that it? Was that all it took, a blood sacrifice? If Anton had known, he would have gladly opened up a vein to set them free.

From his mother's perspective, he was only gone ten minutes. Ten minutes later he had lost twenty pounds and had gained a friend bleeding from a deep gash in his stomach. They were both rushed to the hospital. The last time Anton saw Eric was when he was being wheeled out of surgery to the ICU.

Anton recovered, at least physically. Everyone recovers physically, eventually, from even the worst things. The boy in class who decided he was gay for knowing too much about French palaces punched him so hard he lost a tooth, but he recovered from that. Eric's father, who decided they had both been bewitched—maybe they stepped on a dwarf mound, maybe Anton's mother forgot to sacrifice a chicken before buying the house, who knows?—handed him a note in his hospital room which said, simply, that Eric wished not to see him again.

And he'd like to believe he recovered from that, too.

Anton graduated from college and now worked in an ad agency, drafting communication plans for various companies, earning good money. Sometimes, a distraught co-worker would go on a rant about a difficult client who kept changing their minds about the color motif for an upcoming event, or a supplier who couldn't seem to follow directions, and he would very nearly say, *At least you're alive. At least you're not stuck in an eight-hundred-room palace with a monster. At least you're not alone.*

One night, while trying to decide what meat to buy at the grocery, someone sidled up to him and said, "Anton?"

Who else would say his name with such hesitation, such fear? Eric's wounds had healed, but he was Eric's walking wound, a reminder.

"Where the hell have you been?" Eric demanded. He looked well, was dressed well. Sneakers with corporate clothing. Maybe he worked in an agency, too. Graphic artist. Anton remembered Eric drawing on the floors of Belshazzar's house with powdered drywall, chipping paint off the walls to reveal a face. It's you, he would say. I'm painting you.

"Why did you leave the hospital without saying goodbye?" Eric looking as if he were bleeding right there, in the grocery aisle. "I've looked all over for you. You're not even on Facebook."

Why did you leave the hospital without saying goodbye?

Anton said nothing, not trusting himself to speak without letting the anger and regret overcome his voice.

Eric sighed. "Do you need to finish your shopping now, or can we get out of here and get a drink?"

My God, Anton thought. Must we now unpack the past twenty years, the lies our parents have told us? Maybe Eric's father saw the way Anton looked at his son, saw the tender way he held his hand. He was weighed and was found wanting.

Perhaps for twenty years he had unknowingly longed for it, the room with Eric in it. Anton stood now in his own impossible place, with its many rooms, and watched it all collapse until he was sure there was only one room he could enter.

When I Die, I Want You to Have All of My Stuff

(1) METALLIC GRAY MESSENGER BAG that I bought when I decided I wanted to go on several solo trips this year. It has RFID blocking slots for your passport and your credit cards, a main compartment that locks, and even a detachable LED light.

(I sound like a salesman just now. Who'd have thought I'd be nostalgic for malls and salespeople???)

There is a padded compartment in the back, and this morning when I slipped my planner in there, I realized that it could also fit that leather-bound notebook that you brought with you everywhere.

I thought, here, I could actually leave you something useful. I imagined you carrying this bag with your leather-bound notebook in it, and it made me happy, as though the bag were eternal life.

(2) NOTEBOOK WITH WATERCOLOR SKETCHES OF BIRDS ENDEMIC TO SOUTHEAST ASIA

which I got in a shop connected to an art museum in Ilocos. Did you know that when I was there, the museum owner dropped by? I always find myself unsatisfied and frustrated with my interactions with people I admire. For example: I told the museum owner that I loved the galleries and it's my first time here! Gushing like a schoolgirl.

It was an inadequate translation of what I really wanted to say—that I love his art, that the view of his garden made me feel alive.

It sounds pretentious but it's true! It's true, and I can't say it, and he just gave me a blank look, probably thinking, Who is this crazy person shaking my hand.

What an awkward moment.

And it got me thinking of my conversations with you.

(3) BLACK LAPTOP BACKPACK with a removable waterproof gray sheet that you can pull out and fit over the bag. The bag itself is waterproof, but just to be sure I guess? It sounds like overkill, but at least it will keep your stuff dry, even during a storm.

I bought that backpack during my trip in Baguio three months ago.

Have I told you about my bus ride to Manila after that trip?

It was nearing sunset, and the bus passed by several rice fields in Tarlac.

Here in the city, the horizon always looks like it's just a corridor's length away, thanks to the thick haze of pollution. But out there in the province there was nothing but field and sky and clouds, as far as the eye can see.

The smell of manure was so strong it penetrated the windows of the air-conditioned bus.

A second later, without warning, the smell of shit was replaced by the smell of smoke, the stench of a long-ago fire.

Have I told you about this?

I would never forget the sky that day.

The torched rice fields, those splotches of black for miles and miles. Like bruises.

I didn't think much of it. I thought it was just emergency field burning, like what they do during a serious insect infestation.

They say now that the fire started in one of the houses in the area, in the house of the first family that got sick.

They burned their house first, then their palay. Then themselves. Of course the fire spread with the wind.

The news kept saying they went insane, but it doesn't affect your brain, right? Just your lungs and your heart.

But I didn't know this yet at the time, and so when I look at the backpack I am reminded not of the burned fields of Tarlac, but of Baguio, of my bus ride up there, of the houses carved into the faces of the mountains.

I would like to go back there.

(4) SILK SCARF WITH PEACOCK PRINT that I purchased in Hanoi. This was before the quarantine.

I haggled with a woman manning the stall at the street market, and she said that even if I bought a hundred of her items she wouldn't cut the price, because she is tired and she has been up since early that morning, don't I know?

I ended up paying the full price because I got embarrassed by the drama. Ha-ha.

I joined a group tour and stayed there for three days.

On the third day, while staring at Ha Long Bay's limestone pillars, I started making lists in my head of tasks I had to begin at the office the next day, and I found myself getting annoyed.

Back to reality, they always say. So what is this? A dream? Back to dreaming for me, really, because I was unhappy at my job. Back to sleepwalking.

And so there I was, sitting on a boat in the Gulf of Tonkin, getting annoyed that in a few hours I would have to get back to work.

But I should have been grateful, you know? Grateful that the pillars were there, grateful that I had the means and the energy to see them.

My worries and my irritation clouded the precious few hours I had left in a beautiful place I would never be able to visit again.

You used to say that I was never truly present, and I never understood what you meant. Until now.

If only I could have those hours back.

I should have been grateful for every joy I have ever experienced, no matter how brief.

(5) FITTED BEANIE that I bought for my now-canceled trip to Seoul, planned way ahead of this mess.

I have never experienced autumn. It looks beautiful in the pictures. Plus: South Korea is a safe zone! If your tests are negative you can actually fly there. You should, you know.

This beanie is damn expensive, can I just say?! However the tag says it has "heat-capturing" lining, so I hope it's worth the price.

The guys here at the clinic will have these things sanitized and wrapped, and they'll place them in a box with your name on it.

One of the nurses promised to track you down.

I hope she finds you.

I hope she finds you safe, and healthy, and I hope you'll accept this box from her.

Love,

WHERE YOU ARE NOW IS BETTER THAN WHERE YOU WERE BEFORE

The office reminded Lily of the quirky, industrial interior of co-working spaces back home in Manila: white brick walls, empty beer crates turned into chairs in the lounge, copywriters pinning paper on clotheslines or writing their ideas on the glass partitions with silver markers (*IDEA—Execution—Execution—Execution*). One of the teams was working on a pitch for a juice company— their "idea clothesline" filled with sketches of oranges— and Evie the art director was holding her head, sighing and saying to anyone within earshot, "This project is giving me a migraine."

"You're the new office assistant?" said Andrea, Evie's partner for the juice company pitch, an Australian accent sailing out of her mouth. Andrea was the only other Southeast Asian-looking person in the office, and dressed exactly like the kind of person who would work in an office like this. White jacket over a black tulle dress, lavender hair pinned back with unicorn hair clips. Peter told Lily in the interview that "every day is casual Friday", and so she came to work wearing jeans and sneakers and a white blouse. But, next to Andrea, she felt almost formal. Old-fashioned.

"That's me," Lily said.

Andrea leaned in, whispered, "Pinoy ka?"

"Yes," Lily said, startled.

"Me too!" Andrea said.

"Have you lived here long?"

Andrea giggled as though Lily had given her a compliment. "I've only been here a year."

"But your accent—"

"It just makes it easier for people to understand me," she said. "When I worked at a BPO back home, we had courses to neutralize our accents, get that American twang in there. Same principle." She rested her hip on the side of the printer, placed an elbow on top of the pile of paper Lily was collating. "And you? Have you been in Sydney long?"

"I've been here a couple of months," Lily said, eyeing the pile Andrea was on the verge of tipping over.

"You should try it," Andrea said.

"Try what?"

"You know. Neutralizing your accent."

"I like my accent," Lily said. "I think people understand me just fine."

"Okay," Andrea said.

They didn't have the chance to speak again the rest of that morning, and Lily was grateful for it, happy to be alone in her small cubicle in the corner, doodling notes on discarded paper (*IDEA-Execution-Execution*), while Andrea and Evie brainstormed in front of the clothesline. Evie was a head taller than Andrea, and seemed to loom over her as she said, repeatedly, "I don't know, A. It's just not working."

"Why don't we try it this way?" Andrea said, doodling something on a paper pinned on the clothesline. "Revise this part here and see how it flows."

Evie massaged her temples. "Okay, give me a few," she said. "I need to take something for this headache."

Andrea walked to Lily's table. "You want to head out for lunch somewhere?"

Evie swept past them, stern-faced, in her shiny leather pants and her high-heeled boots, and Lily found herself saying, "Sure."

Andrea took her to a self-serve hotpot restaurant. Majority of the clientele were East Asian international students, and as they were enveloped in simultaneous conversations carried out in Mandarin and Japanese, Andrea shed her accent and spoke in Filipino, asking Lily about her first day. Lily found it pleasant to talk to her, until Andrea said, "What's taking you so long? Don't worry about it, lunch is on me."

They were standing in front of the lit shelves, and Lily was taking a moment to look at each of the ingredients. Each bowl would be weighed at the end of the line, and Lily realized, with angry dismay, that Andrea thought she was taking a while to choose because she was calculating the price of the meal in her head. Andrea was acting like the worldly older sister taking a poor, provincial lass around the big, bad city and Lily wanted to say, *Listen here, I have my own money, I can manage on my own, don't patronize me,* but decided against it. Instead, she took the heaviest ingredients she could find—beef balls, cheese-filled fish cakes, tofu—and stood next to Andrea as the bowls were weighed. Andrea's bowl was ten dollars.

"Seventeen dollars for this one," the cashier said.

"Whoa!" Andrea said, taking out her wallet. "Someone's hungry." Lily shrugged and flashed the sweetest smile she could muster.

They sat next to the windows. The restaurant was crowded, and Lily could feel every jostle and shudder of the group of young men sitting behind her, laughing over a joke. "Hey," Andrea called over to them. "Can you be careful? You're hitting my friend over here."

The group apologized and Andrea switched back to Filipino. "The soup's good, huh?" Andrea said.

"Yes. Thank you."

"I heard from Peter we're attending the same uni."

"Yes, I'm taking a diploma course. English Studies."

"Ugh. Shakespeare, right?"

"Not just Shakespeare but—" Lily started saying, and just gave up. "Yeah. Sure."

"Do you have family in Sydney?" Andrea asked.

"No. You?"

"No," Andrea said. Then: "I came here with my girlfriend."

"Oh, cool."

Andrea didn't say anything more.

"Is she also in advertising?" Lily asked.

"No." Andrea ran her chopsticks through the soup, searching for the remaining noodles and fish cakes. "Are you keeping up with the news back home?" She mentioned the Australian missionary who had been working in the

Philippines for three decades and who was suddenly deported after she criticised the President. The police announcing that 4,500 people had been shot dead in the government's anti-drug operations—"And that's just the official number." Andrea sighed. "It feels as if things are just getting worse, aren't they? Last year, Paula and I finally decided we should do what we've long planned to do, work and study abroad. She enrolled in Science and I got into Marketing. I got a job here after three weeks."

"That was quick."

Andrea nodded. "I was lucky. Paula had a harder time. She taught in UP for years. Suddenly she couldn't even get an interview. Day after day she would talk about how hard it was to keep hoping, how demoralized she felt." She paused, staring out the window. "I think she started to resent me as well, towards the end."

"Oh," Lily said. "You broke up?"

Andrea turned her focus back to Lily. "One time, Paula told me, 'Do you know that the observable universe is 93 billion light-years wide? Which means it would take 93 billion years for the light of a star to travel from one end of the universe to the other. My life feels like such a small, ridiculous thing to worry about, when you think about that.' Do you know what I said? I said, 'Finding a job here may be such an infinitesimal achievement when compared to the vastness of the universe, but it would certainly help stop you from whining.'"

From the counter, the Chinese cashier called the orders for pick-up, every number sounding like a hopeful question. *Sixty-four? Thirty-eight?*

"I'm so sorry," Lily said.

Andrea pushed her bowl away. "So tell me," she said, "where do you live? Do you live in a flat-share?"

Lily gave her address. "I live downstairs from my landlady, but I have my own entrance through the basement."

Andrea frowned. "Is your landlady named Marie?"

"You know Marie?" Lily said. "She messaged me about the flat on Flatmates. I didn't even want to go at first because it was so cheap."

"You were thinking there has got to be a catch."

"I mean, wouldn't you? Of course, if you convert the rent amount to pesos the amount is still staggering, but it's really cheap for the area."

"Did Marie tell you anything else about the flat?" Andrea asked. "About the former tenant?"

"No," Lily said. "Don't tell me someone died in there."

Andrea didn't speak for a moment.

"What?" Lily said.

"What?" Andrea said, but said nothing else.

IDEA: Where you are now is better than where you were before.

Execution:
A woman in her late 20s moves into her new flat in Sydney. To get to it, she has to go through two doors in the basement: the main basement door, and the garage door to the unit. The garage

door rattles as it moves up, the slow, raucous
ascent revealing her landlady's gray sedan.

The flat has a cast iron doorstopper in the shape
of a reclining dog. She nudges the dog into place
and takes off her shoes, stows them away in
the rack outside, locks the door behind her.

The flat is small and has no demarcations—two
steps from the bed and she is at the dining table,
six steps and she is in the kitchen, eight steps and
she is in the shower. The blue carpet has a lighter
patch next to the glass door going out into the
courtyard, the fiber fading under the sunlight. She
slides the door open, feeling the bite of the wind
on her bare legs. The wind also brings with it a
sharp, musky scent, and she notices the potted tree
roses, yellow and dying. Beyond the flowers—a
sliver of sky, the disembodied heads and voices
of people walking up there on the sidewalk.

All mine, she thinks, and she smiles, happy
for the first time in a long time.

Execution:
The woman can speak and write English well,
but often feels as if she has to scale an invisible
barrier whenever she interacts with people.

(Montage)

• At her first job interview in Sydney for a copywriting job, the hiring manager asks, *I don't mean to offend, but where did you learn to speak English so well?* even as her resume sits between them, beaming with promise. *Work Experience: Senior Copywriter (6 years).* She does not get the job, the company explaining that they need an Australian citizen or permanent resident to fill the role. As she accumulates rejections, she wonders if she has made a grave mistake coming here, if she should perhaps tame her ambitions.

• *Where are you from?* her classmates ask. *The Philippines.* And they nod and say *Okay* and she wonders what they are picturing in their heads. White sand beaches? Policemen pulling a teenage boy down an alley and leaving him dead near a pigsty?

• The woman at the counter at Coles is Filipino, and she says, *You should try to stay here after your course. Everything's expensive in Sydney, but you'll earn good money. Better than back home, anyway.* Money always comes up, whenever she speaks to Filipino workers here. *I'm doing this for personal growth,* she wants to say, but—is that it? The words feel inadequate and insincere. *I'm here because with the state of politics back home I was starting to feel like a monster, treating kindness as if it were a finite thread that I have to hold on to, to keep from unravelling. But I still can't loosen my grasp.* The woman at the counter says, "That will be forty dollars," and she extracts the still-unfamiliar bills, shoves the words back down her throat.

• *Did you also work as an office assistant back home?*
someone asks at the temp agency, and she considers
this question that is only a question, that should not
sting. And yet it stings. *No,* she replies, barbed wire
in her voice, and an awful silence sets in, and that is
the end of the conversation.

Execution:
Her mother calls her. She accepts the call but does
not turn on the video, making an excuse that her Wi-
Fi isn't stable. *You're in Australia and you're Wi-Fi isn't
stable?* Before she can think of another excuse, her
mother makes a comment again about how beautiful
it must be in Sydney. *Did you get a job in an ad agency,
like your old job here? They're paying you well, I hope?*

Then it is something about needing money to fix
the roof, *a portion of the roof in the kitchen got blown
off during the storm, did your brother tell you*—the
woman cuts her mother off, explaining to her again
that she's not earning that much, she is here to
study, and *haven't I told you this several times before?*

A pregnant pause from four thousand miles away,
and the woman takes a deep breath, bracing herself.
We're proud of you, of course, her mother says, *but
don't let this get to your head. Remember your family. You
can't be selfish. Your father and I don't even understand
why you took English in UP and English again in
Sydney. You should have just applied for a hotel job in
Dubai like what your Uncle Ricky told you last year.*

Execution:
She takes note of the things the former tenant has
left behind, or has abandoned: rice vinegar, oyster
sauce, a chipped mug, a scorched pan. Mounted
on the wall next to the door is a whiteboard
with half-erased marks and an encircled list
(*rent, Optus Recharge, Opal, groceries*) of budget
items. She means to erase it but the circle makes
her hesitate, as if the list were a memorial.

Sometimes at night she feels an oppressive
weight on her chest, and wonders if this is also
something that belongs to the former tenant, this
feeling of *I wish I didn't have to leave home*, left
here with the 5-cup rice cooker, with the seven-
dollar toaster from K-Mart. Or is this one of the
few things in this flat that belongs to her?

AFTER THEY GOT back from lunch, Andrea walked
the length of the office calling for Evie. She was not in
her cubicle or in any of the breakout rooms. "Have you
seen Evie?" Andrea said, stopping by Lily's table a few
minutes later. Andrea looked frazzled, angry. "We have to
present to Peter in thirty minutes and she hasn't done the
revisions I asked for."

Lily had not seen Evie. She went to the pantry to
wash her coffee mug, and saw a pair of high-heeled boots
sticking out from behind the refrigerator. "Hello?" she
said, and jumped when Andrea burst into the room.

"I swear, Evie doesn't respect me," Andrea said. "The one time I wanted to take charge of a pitch idea and she—what are you doing?"

Lily was approaching the boots. They belonged to Evie, sitting slumped on the floor, forehead resting against the side of the refrigerator. Lily knelt in front of her, touched her knee, shook her. Evie didn't move.

"Shit," Andrea said, and ran out of the pantry shouting for help.

PETER TOLD LILY she could leave work early, and so she did, not stopping to talk to anyone. When she got home, there was a woman in a beige coat waiting in front of the garage door. "Hello," Lily said, uncertain.

"Hi," the woman said. The woman had brown skin, jet-black hair tied in a loose bun. "I'm just waiting for someone."

Lily thought she could detect a soft Filipino accent, but she wasn't sure, so she just spoke to her in English. "Do you want to wait inside?" She wasn't thinking straight. She could still feel Evie's leather pants beneath her fingers, hear the sound they made against the sheet when the EMTs lifted her to the gurney.

The woman followed her through the garage door, past Marie's car, and as Lily turned her key in the lock, she felt her Manila sensibilities return. She nudged the dog doorstopper into place with her right foot, ready to pick it up and use it as a weapon in case this stranger tried something.

"So, uh," Lily said, "you'll just wait for Marie out here?" Did the woman even mention Marie by name?

The woman glanced past her, and Lily followed her gaze. The woman was looking at the whiteboard.

"You haven't erased the list." The woman smiled, her hands deep in the pockets of her coat. "Just write over the words again with a whiteboard marker. That will make them easier to erase."

"Right," Lily said.

"Right," the woman said. She turned away, and Lily closed the door.

LILY LAY IN bed and stayed in the same position for hours.

She must have fallen asleep at some point. She woke up suddenly and found the woman in the beige coat sitting at the foot of her bed.

"Do you know that the observable universe is 93 billion light-years wide?" the woman said.

"I actually do know that," Lily said. "Somebody told me."

"Do you know what's important in life?"

"Money," Lily said without hesitation.

"Really?" the woman said, looking intrigued.

"You know," Lily said, "after I graduated from college, I didn't even think about leaving the Philippines. Everyone said I should, that I would earn more abroad. I thought—" She laughed, embarrassed. "I thought it meant something, deciding to stay. I thought I could give back. And now people are getting shot on the street, and

I have no savings left, and I can't even afford to help my mother." Lily laughed again, harder this time. "I don't know what to do anymore."

The woman glanced at the list on the whiteboard. "Money's not what's important in life," she said.

"It's not?" Lily realized there were tears in her eyes. When did that happen?

"It's not," the woman said. She seemed so sure of it.

A KNOCK ON the door. Lily opened her eyes and glanced at her phone. It was seven p.m. She stood up with a groan, and opened the door to find Andrea standing outside with a large thermos.

"Did Marie let you in?" Lily asked.

Andrea lifted the flask. "Do you want some goon?"

"Do I want some what?"

"Goon," Andrea said. "That's what Australians call boxed wine. It's vile, but it's cheap."

"Why is it called 'goon'?"

"Who the hell knows?" Andrea said. "I wanted to check up on you. You suddenly disappeared from the office." She sighed and sat on the floor, her back to the door. "Evie's in the ICU. Blood clot in her brain."

"Jesus." Lily closed the door and sat down next to her. The garage smelled faintly of petrol.

"And to think just a few hours before that we were having a fight about orange juice," Andrea said. "Orange juice! Arguing about it like it's the most important thing in life. Really puts things into perspective." She sighed. "I thought I already learned this lesson. But I guess I didn't. Or I did and I forgot."

"What do you mean?"

"Marie didn't let me in," Andrea said, and showed her a garage door key. "I let myself in. Marie must have forgotten that Paula and I have a copy each. I really ought to return it but I keep—"

"You used to live here?"

"Paula died here six months ago," Andrea said.

It took a while for things to click into place. *Did Marie tell you anything else about the flat?*

"Oh, God," Lily said.

"Heart attack," Andrea said. "'Undiagnosed heart condition'. That's what the doctor said." She looked sheepish. "Are you thinking of moving out now? Sorry, Marie really should have told you. But don't move out! It's a good flat. Paula loved the roses in the courtyard."

Andrea took another swig from the flask. "Can I tell you something really crazy? Sometimes I get so drunk I forget that she's died, and I would go down here and just stand around, waiting for her. Then after about an hour it would hit me, and—" She laughed, but the laughter soon turned into a deep sigh, a shaky breath.

"Sorry," Lily said, not knowing what else to say.

Andrea chugged down her drink and wiped her lips. "This will sound weird, and you can say no, but can I look inside?"

Inside the flat, Andrea walked unsteadily on the carpet. "Everything looks the same," she marvelled in a soft voice, glancing out at the courtyard. "Oh, but the roses are dying."

"I don't know anything about flowers," Lily said.

They ended up looking at the whiteboard with the encircled list. Lily imagined spending her last moments staring at a list of things that seemed so significant they crowded out everything else but, in the grand scheme of things, did not even matter at all.

But then she thought of her mother, the comfortable future her family was hoping she could provide, their country crashing down around their ears. She understood that light from one end of the universe would take 93 billion years to travel to the opposite end, and that by then the planet would be dust, with no nations, no wars, no people shot on the street. She understood this, and yet her daily worries felt heavy, as though they would be there until the end of time.

Andrea said, "You haven't erased the list."

The remark had a ring of familiarity to it.

Andrea stared at the whiteboard, looking helpless, hopeless.

Do you know what's important in life?

Back home, Lily could feel herself becoming monstrous, treating kindness as if it were a finite thread that she had to hold on to, to keep from unravelling.

"Do you want to talk about it?" Lily asked, loosening her grasp. "Head out, grab something to eat?"

Andrea turned to her. "Really?" she said. "Okay."

"Okay," Lily said.

"The team might visit Evie this weekend. Do you want to join? We're carpooling."

"Sure."

Andrea pointed at the board. "May I?"

Lily grabbed a table napkin and the whiteboard marker and handed them to Andrea. Andrea wrote carefully over the list, tracing the words that had hardened on the whiteboard so they could be easily erased. In their place, she wrote, *Visit Evie w/ team - Sat,* and, after a brief pause, *Google how to take care of roses.*

Lily laughed and followed Andrea out of the flat, closing the door behind her.

1:40 AM

Before the man with a gun entered the convenience store, Grace was sitting alone at a sticky, soda-splattered table, her broken arm throbbing like a heart, the roof of her mouth burning from the coffee she had drunk too quickly. It was nearly two in the morning, and there were only three other people in the store. The cashier sitting behind the counter was playing some game on his phone and having an expletive-laden argument with it. There were two men facing each other at the table behind her. She had glanced up and had made a swift assessment (cute, also cute; dead-tired and wary, alert and looking like he's making lists in his head) when they came in earlier, talking about a taxi driver who had tried to swindle them or something. The alert-looking one was wearing a mauve rubber wristband. An Institute guest, so the other guy probably worked for the Institute. Grace knew about the wristband because she and the rest of her class wore it when they toured the facility last month. Researchers from the Institute made her nervous. Who knew what kind of experiments they were doing up there?

The convenience store was near Grace's house. She would have gone to a coffee shop but realized she didn't have enough money. She wanted to sit somewhere quiet, where she could think about Alice and the car crash, and the fact that it was Alice's birthday today, and that in fifty years, if Grace would be so fortunate, Grace would be dead, and in another fifty years after that, maybe everyone who had ever known Alice would be dead, and there would be no one left to remember or mourn her, and so every person or thing or memory, no matter how bright or searing, no matter how kind or painful, could be defeated by time, and could disappear as though it had never even existed.

Grace was crying. Because she couldn't even toast Alice on her birthday with a good cup of coffee, because fifty years felt at once too long and too short. She was aware only of her pain and her grief, so when the man with a gun rushed into the store, she didn't look up, and so didn't see what was happening until the cashier and the man got into a loud argument, loud enough to make Grace stop thinking about Alice. There was a crash, a sudden flash of fluorescence as broken glass from the lights showered the grocery shelves, a shout ("Get down!"), and Grace was down, lying flat on her back on the cold floor (*How did that happen*, she thought idly), and the two men from the Institute were bending over her, the dead-tired one taking off his jacket and pressing it to her chest. Her chest felt warm but her hands were so cold. The man with the mauve wristband, as though reading her mind, held her hand, touched her face.

"You'll be okay," he said, and *Oh, Alice, Grace* thought. *Is this it, then?*

"FASCINATING."

"Excuse me?" Peter glanced at his watch. It was 1:40 a.m.. Sitting across the table was John, or so the Director said. To Peter, "John" sounded like a safe, monosyllabic code word. The Institute was big on codes—like *NTW, need to know,* which was what they told him when he asked who John was and Peter refused to just accept their uncomplicated answer ("He's the Director's guest"). Which meant the wristband they had slapped on John was not just a visitor's ID but also a tracker and a vital signs scanner, and this babysitting job was no babysitting job but a scientific investigation way, way, *way* beyond his pay grade.

Peter wondered what the experiment was. Behavior modification, sleep deprivation, a drug trial of some sort? He wouldn't be surprised; he'd seen and spoken with John for two weeks now inside the Institute and he sounded high most of the time. But wasn't this a bit atypical (and dangerous) to just let the subject go to an uncontrolled environment? Yes, with a researcher, sure, but—

Or maybe, Peter thought, the team decided to just give him a break. God knows he was sick to death of making notes about the stupid mice.

Yes.

Sure.

An instruction like, "John wants to go out. Take him where he wants to go and come back around 3 a.m." does *not* a romantic date make, he thought.

But he is good-looking. Peter smiled, and shook his head.

"You don't remember?" John said, startling him.

"Remember what?"

"Fascinating," John said again, looking around at the empty tables, the girl with her arm in a sling, the cashier swearing at his phone behind the counter.

"It appears that space-time here has no chronology protection," John said, with a look of wonder. Peter mirrored the smile even though he couldn't understand a word. "It is completely malleable. Or did I somehow simply trigger a jump back in time, in my moment of weakness and fear, and this is not the same universe, but simply a universe that runs parallel to the other, where the girl—"

John stopped talking. He turned on his seat, looked at the girl, at the glass doors.

"What is it?" Peter said, and to his horror John stood up and walked over to where the girl was sitting.

"No," Peter said, standing up. "Wait. *Shit.*" But John was already talking to the girl.

"Hello," John said, and sat on the plastic chair beside her. The chairs were bolted to the floor, so the girl couldn't move hers away, so she just *leaned* away, looking frightened and unsure.

"Hello?" she said, glancing at Peter, who had stopped at a safe distance.

"Don't be frightened," John said, and Peter covered his face with his hand and groaned, because those three words just moved the conversation into creepy man/pedophile territory. The girl knew it, too. She looked about ready to bolt.

"How are you?" John said.

"I'm fine, I guess." She glanced at Peter again, and Peter nearly said, *No. No. I don't know this person. Stop looking at me.*

"Do you remember me?" John said, and gestured toward Peter. "Us?"

The girl frowned, and Peter moved closer to grab John's arm. "No?" she said. "Am I supposed to?"

"I suppose not," John said.

"Sorry," Peter told the girl, and pulled John away from the table and a possible lawsuit. They settled on a pair of chairs near the glass doors.

"What the hell was that?" Peter said.

"I just wanted to check something," John said.

"Maybe we should leave."

"No!" John said it so forcefully that Peter jumped. "No," John repeated, in a softer voice. "Let's stay. I want to see what happens next."

A minute later the glass doors banged open and in came a large man in a jacket with an expression on his face that spelled trouble. He walked straight to the counter, and prodded the cashier in the chest with his finger. The cashier stood up, leaving his phone squawking near the cash register, and walked around the counter to face the man. Peter couldn't hear what they were talking about, but it was clear they were arguing.

Peter said, "I think we need to—"

Get out of here, was what he wanted to say, but before he could finish his sentence, he heard something shatter, and he realized in the second that followed that *The man has a gun!—The girl!*—and "Get down!" Peter shouted, and the man with the gun was running out the doors and the cashier was kneeling on the floor with his hands over his head.

The girl was bleeding from her chest. "Call an ambulance!" Peter shouted at the pale-faced cashier, and he took off his jacket and placed it on the girl's wound.

Oh God, Peter thought. *Oh God, this poor girl will die here. And we don't even know her name.* "My name's Peter," he said. "And that's John. What's your name, sweetheart?"

John took the girl's hand in his. "You'll be okay," he said.

PETER GLANCED AT his watch. It was 1:40 a.m. John (if that was even his real name) was staring at his hands. Cute. Too short and too jumpy for Peter's taste, but sitting with him beat watching mice solve a puzzle for the 300th time.

"What did they tell you about me?" John asked, fiddling with the mauve wristwatch, tracing the Institute's logo with his forefinger.

"Not much," Peter said. "They said you're the Director's guest."

"'Guest'," John echoed with distaste. "That's the word they used, huh."

"Are you okay?"

John looked at him for a long moment, long enough to make Peter shift in his seat.

"Are you happy with your life?" John asked.

Peter laughed in surprise. "*What?*"

"Is there something in your past that you want to change? An action you want to reverse? A death you want to prevent?"

There was this boy once, Peter wanted to say. *But then there is always this boy once, isn't it.* "Why?" he said. "Are you going to tell me you're a time traveler?"

John smiled and looked at his hands again. Peter found his smile both pleasant and unnerving. *Christ, get a grip.*

"Why did you want to come here?" Peter asked.

John seemed offended. "I didn't choose to come here." Then: "Oh, you meant *here,* the store."

Of course, I meant the damn store.

"It's bright," John said, looking up at the lights. "And quiet."

Peter looked past him and saw the girl at the next table bent over her coffee, crying. He wondered if he should speak to her. But it could be something personal, family or boy trouble; she would hate him for his intrusion. Then he noticed her arm in a sling, and wondered if she were in pain.

"That girl's crying," Peter said. John glanced over a shoulder. When he stood up to approach her, John looked alarmed.

"Wait," he said. "Don't—"

Peter stood across the table from her and leaned forward. "Hello," he said. "I'm sorry—does your arm hurt? Do you need a doctor?"

Moments later Peter was lying on his side on the floor, his nose filling with the metallic smell of his own blood. He couldn't feel his legs.

"I can't feel my legs," he said, and burst into tears. John knelt beside him. He could hear the girl sobbing, the cashier screaming for an ambulance on the phone. "You'll be okay," John said. The terror and pain dissipated for a few moments as Peter felt surprise—awe, wonder—upon seeing the tears on John's face. The last thing Peter felt before blacking out was John's hand in his.

"WHAT TIME IS it?"

Peter glanced at his watch. "One-forty."

John nodded. He looked around. There was the girl with her arm in a sling, the cashier screaming at a gadget in his hands. Peter. Same as always. John wondered if the men back at the Institute were getting any interesting readings on their instruments. A spike of energy? A disappearance? A momentary burst of static as the universe changed stations?

John had the urge to just tear off this primitive tracker from his wrist, but he knew that if he did a black car would swing into the lot and drag him back to the laboratory. They were the ones who brought him here; it must follow that they were the only ones who could help him go back home.

If they would let him go back home.

If they even knew how.

And yet: he couldn't leave yet. Not with what was about to come to pass.

"What a marvelous thing limited consciousness is," he said. Peter threw him that look he always gave him, that go-on-and-humor-me half-squint.

"It makes you blind beyond a trivial context," John continued. "For example, the larger context is this: sixty countries, involving 495 groups and militias, are in conflict on this planet. Six hundred and thirteen species of underwater fauna have just died in the past eleven seconds. Thirty-seven hundred stars are dead—have died—are dying—in a galaxy 13 billion light-years away from here. And yet just moments earlier you managed to focus your anger at this man, a stranger, who rebuffed us."

"Listen—that taxi driver is a dick. It's against the law to—"

"I don't consider it a flaw. You have the capacity to make your world smaller, and yet make it remain as massive, as important, as the world itself. It's an incredible thing."

"Like love?" Peter laughed, but he looked disconcerted.

Love. John smiled. "Yes," he said. "Perhaps. Perhaps love can only be felt by beings with limited consciousness. If you love everything then it is as if you love nothing. With a limited consciousness, you have no choice but to love one thing, at most a handful of things, and derive fulfilment from them, but also feel wretched and inadequate all your life, for if you lose that one thing, what will be left?"

He looked toward the glass doors.

"Every single moment can collapse into one moment," he said. "One hundred seventy billion galaxies collapsing into the barrel of a gun."

"John—"

John turned to him. Peter looked like he was trying to decide whether to speak or not.

"What is it?" John said.

Peter looked around the store. "I don't know," he said. "I feel like I just got hit by a massive dose of déjà vu. Has that ever happened to you?"

John turned his head and saw the girl looking at him.

"Do you remember me?" he said.

The girl looked hesitant to speak, but at last she said, "Is your name John?"

So not a parallel universe then.

The same *universe.*

I can't be the one doing this, John thought. *Another force is at hand.*

What is going on?

There was an umbrella stand next to the glass doors. John stood up—to Peter's protestations—grabbed an umbrella, and slipped it into the door handles. The cashier shouted a warning, a challenge, and walked around the counter, but stopped walking when John began pushing one of the tables to block the doors. From the corner of his eye he could see the girl standing with a hand over her mouth, Peter walking briskly and stopping a few feet away from him, like the cashier, like the way you stand away from something you don't understand. Something that terrifies you.

"John," Peter said. "What are you—"

"We need to get out of here," John said. The cashier turned on his heel and ran back to the counter. John followed him. He felt Peter's hand on his arm but he shook him off. "Listen to me. Someone with a weapon is going to go through those doors in a few minutes. An angry man. Someone you know."

"What's wrong with your friend?" the cashier asked Peter. He had his hands inside a drawer, rummaging through the papers and knickknacks there.

"Listen to me!" John said, slamming a hand on the counter. The cashier jumped. The girl let out a soft, frightened whimper. "Someone's going to die if you don't—"

The cashier lifted his hands, and in his hand was a gun.

Ah, John thought. He stepped back from the counter, slowly.

Horror vacui, *they always say.*

But also: Horror paradoxa.

"Wait," Peter said, pleading. The girl had started to cry. "Wait, listen, why don't we all calm down? I know this guy. He's not dangerous."

"Then get him out of here," the cashier said.

That's what this universe is trying to do, John thought, and he nearly smiled. *It's okay. I am not from here. I am not supposed to be here.* Horror paradoxa. *It's just the cosmos rooting me out.*

"John," Peter said. "Come on. I think you just need some sleep. Let's get out of here."

John lunged at the cashier's neck, closing the gap, making sure there wouldn't be space for Peter or the girl to jump into, and the gun went off, as expected, the bullet finding its home. Someone screamed, perhaps the girl. John fell to the floor, hard, and he felt the heat spreading outward from his chest, felt the pain like a planet crushing his ribs.

He saw Peter's face as he knelt beside him, felt his hands applying pressure to the wound to staunch the bleeding. *This is unfair,* John thought then, grasping at Peter's hands slippery with his blood, despairing and at the same time marveling at the novelty of this emotion. *I did not even ask to be here.*

John began to cry. "Shit," Peter said, face crumbling, but he swiped at his eyes with his arm and his gaze turned to steel. "Listen," he said, and John listened, and all of the world became Peter's voice, saying, "You'll be okay."

FORTITUDE

The grimy announcement board at the corner of Lakandula and Marilag said *10th Anniversary of the P-40i Settlement. Festivities in the Fortitude Plaza. Glory to Bathala!* followed by *Tuesday, 10th of June, 36 deg C* followed by *Thirty past the hour of Five.* Sara glanced at her phone and nodded. Seconds later she saw a woman in a black shirt appearing from the bend and approaching the intersection in slow steps. Sara placed the box on her lap and watched her, and waited. The woman, tall and lean like bamboo, seemed to be favoring her right side. The woman stopped for a moment to look around her, marveling at the state the properties were in.

Sara couldn't blame her. Nature came as a permanent settler in her neighborhood when residents started leaving a decade ago for the nearby planet. Apartment buildings were abandoned and opened their doors to wild dogs. Houses collapsed inward like tin cans in a hot oven. The house where Sara was waiting looked like it had given birth to a tree. Its leaves burst through the roof and branches broke through the windows and the front door. The house's walls had been spray-painted with graffiti— various messages in various languages, all nothing but faint shapes now on the weathered wood. A friend of hers used to live there. Jemima. Now Jemima and her extended family (grandparents, uncles and aunts, her father who petitioned her and her mother) lived in a gated subdivision on P-40i, or Forty, or Fortitude. They had to call it something pleasant, something more than a bunch of letters and numbers, so Fortitude it was.

Sara looked up. The planet was more visible now that the sunlight was starting to fade. Fortitude glowed green against the pink sky.

"Are you Sara?" the woman said, standing in the middle of the road. She could actually lie there on the asphalt if she wanted; no vehicle passed this way anymore. Sara shifted her legs, and Jemima's front porch steps creaked beneath her.

"You're Del?"

"I guess I am." Del approached her and sat one step down. The wood groaned. "This is not going to break, is it?"

Del had a tattoo on her neck. Two black swords. Sara wondered what it meant. Del leaned her back against the railing and took a deep breath.

"Are you hurt?"

"I'm fine," Del said, and took out her card. "It's just incredibly hot tonight. Here."

Sara took her card and swiped it on her phone. *Credit collected*, the screen announced. Sara handed back her card along with the box.

"Here's your phone," Sara said with a smile.

Del thanked her and opened the box. She took out the gadget and placed it on her lap next to her old phone, a battered, thicker model.

She seemed pleased as she swapped the info chips. "This is an improvement," she said. "Thanks."

Del's new phone came alive with a triumphant ding. "Ow."

Del bent forward, tugging at the back of her shirt. "Sorry about this," she said, "but my shoulder—I can't reach back. Can you—"

Del was handing her a compress. "Hot or cold?" Sara asked.

"Cold, for the love of."

Sara pressed the blue button and lifted the back of Del's shirt.

Del was wearing a Transplant, the device covering her left side, from the base of her neck to below her ribs. Her left lung shone a bright yellow-green, its glow pulsating with her every breath.

The skin on the small of Del's back was black with bruises. Sara pressed the compress on it, and Del moaned.

"Thanks," Del said. "You don't seem fazed by my android lung." She chuckled weakly.

"Jemima has an arm Transplant. She's a friend of mine. The skin around it was tender for months."

"Tell me about it." Del moved back and secured the compress in place between her body and the porch step. "Would you mind if we sat here for a bit?"

"I don't mind."

"How old are you, Sara?"

"Thirteen."

"You live here?"

"Yes. You?"

"No."

"Good for you," Sara said.

Up and down the streets in her neighborhood were appliances and furniture left behind on the front lawns, like the merchandise of a perpetual garage sale. *For Sale*, the sign said on every other house, the sign painted or handwritten or rendered in electronic text like the announcement board. On her own street they had only three neighbors left, all old and childless, all too poor to afford to sell their house for one-tenth of its original price, which was the only amount it was going to fetch, because who would want to live here anymore?

"So," Del said, closing her eyes. Sara felt the night breeze on her face. "I'm guessing you also want to migrate to Fortitude."

The planet winked in the distance, as green as Del's lung.

"My brother's there now," Sara said. "He got there just two weeks ago. He has a Work Visa," she added, stressing this.

"Relax. I'm not from Immigration."

"It took him a year to find a company to sponsor him. And to think he already has a Master's degree."

"Advanced degrees usually don't mean anything on Fortitude. Unless he's an engineer. Or a doctor."

"Yes. I'm thinking I could apply for a Student Visa after high school. Get a scholarship. I could study to become an engineer—or a doctor—then I could join him.

Or he could apply to be a resident, and he could petition us."

"So you don't really want to stay here anymore."

"There aren't any good jobs. It's hard to earn money."

"You sound older than you are," Del said. "Is that every child's motivation now when they go to school? To get to Fortitude as quickly as possible and earn money?"

Sara shrugged. "This place sucks."

Del said nothing.

After a moment the woman asked, "How about the Fortitude Bombing of '69? Doesn't that bother you?"

"My mother said it wasn't really a bombing."

"Is that what everyone here believes?"

"I guess."

Del looked saddened by this.

"What I know is two years ago a senator on Fortitude was arrested for bribery," Del said, "and he ordered his supporters to set off a bomb in the plaza during the Anniversary Celebration to divert the public's attention. It worked. A lot of people got injured, even Fortitude's own soldiers, and more than a hundred died. The media covered the bombing every night for several months. The people forgot about the bribery charge, and eventually the senator got released. He's President of the Fourth Quadrant now. Everyone loves him."

"That's what happened?" Sara said. "My mother said it wasn't a bombing, just an explosion from the underground gas line."

Del paused. She took a deep breath and said, slowly, "Well, I wouldn't know for sure. It's all rumors. Maybe your mother was right."

"You've lived on Fortitude, haven't you?"

"How can you possibly know that?"

"You said, is that what everyone *here* believes."

"Ah." Del smiled. "Guilty as charged. I got home just this month."

"Why did you leave?" It was unthinkable for Sara to imagine someone leaving Fortitude for—for this.

"I got homesick." Del removed the compress.

Moments later they were standing on the sidewalk. *Tuesday, 10th of June, 30 deg C, the board said. Twenty past the hour of Six.* A single lamppost, next to the board, glowed on the block. Everything else was in shadows. Sara took out her phone to use as a flashlight.

"Will you be all right going home?" Del asked.

"Yes, I live nearby," Sara said. "Bye now."

"Take care."

Sara walked down the street and turned a sharp left to take her usual shortcut home. The path took her across fields thick with weeds and wildflowers, cats lounging on rocks. Fields that used to be tended gardens. Sometimes she would smell smoke and see people cooking inside homes with no electricity, homes that didn't belong to them. She tried to imagine the place as it was a decade ago. Her parents, newly married and with a baby boy, living in a prosperous neighborhood with good neighbors, a nice school nearby, hardly able to believe their good luck.

The school was torched three months ago and it burned for days.

A man was suddenly in her way. He was wearing camouflage pants and scuffed leather boots. He was drinking from a bottle. An ex-soldier. Sara had seen him around. Always drinking. Always dirty. There were a lot of drunk ex-whatever on this street. Ex-police. Ex-lawyer. Ex-VP of XYZ Company, who couldn't afford to make his car payments anymore.

"Hello," he said. Sara veered to the right but the man blocked her.

"I said hello. Don't be rude."

Sara wondered if she should run.

A knife appeared in the man's hand. He pointed the blade at her eyes.

"I know what you're thinking," he said. Sara's hands shook, making the light from her phone dance. But she was more angry than afraid.

Sara kicked him in the groin. The man fell, dropping his knife and bottle, and Sara heard someone laugh.

"You're a tough girl, aren't you?" Del said, stepping up from behind her. "And here I was, so worried."

The man, writhing and cursing on the ground, glanced up and grimaced. Sara noticed him staring at Del's neck tattoo.

"Well, damn it, girl," he said to Sara, "why didn't you tell me you were with someone from Special Forces? I would have kept my distance if you just said."

Del kicked him in the ribs. The man howled.

"Stay on the ground, soldier," she said, and led Sara away.

Sara realized she was hungry, and so Del led her to a strip mall outside the neighborhood. Sara called home to leave a message for her mother, and they sat down at a fast food restaurant.

"You're a soldier?" Sara asked, and munched on a burger.

"I used to be," Del said. She took out a plastic bottle and shook out two white pills. She chased them down with iced tea. She didn't order any food for herself, just the iced tea.

"I wouldn't have guessed that," Sara said.

Del looked amused. "Why?"

"Aren't you too old to be a soldier?"

Del threw a fry at her, laughing.

"What does Special Forces mean?"

"Oh," Del said, "it's just a fancy name for soldiers stationed on Fortitude. But we just march on parades, salute the Quadrant Presidents. That sort of thing."

That sounded like a lie. That man Del kicked looked scared of her.

"Did you," Sara said, "get that injury at work?"

Del touched her lung, its glow muted by her black shirt, and looked at Sara long and hard before saying, "No."

Sara thought she was lying again.

"Have you always wanted to become a soldier?"

Del sighed and shook her head. "It just happened."

"I don't even know what I want to become," Sara said. "I feel like I won't amount to anything."

Del smiled at this, but her eyes looked like they were mourning for somebody. "Don't worry about it, kid," she said. "It'll get better."

"I just need to get out of here," Sara said. She leaned forward, eager. "Tell me about Fortitude."

Fortitude shone in the sky like a bright star, and Sara imagined living there with her family, enjoying the cold weather, the gleaming buildings, the clean streets. Del glanced outside the window, hand on her steel lung, staring at the green planet with all its lucky people. "It's a beautiful place," she said.

PREMIUM

A man and a woman entered a restaurant and sat in a booth at the back, spending fifteen minutes silently poring over the menu even though they both knew what the other was eventually going to get: braised pork belly, pan-roasted pork, a salad with salted eggs drizzled with sweet vinaigrette, a fruit platter.

The braised pork belly was not available. The man, whose name was Julio, shrugged and said, "Well, we always get that anyway. Time to try something else, I guess." He looked down the list.

"We can just have the fried chicken," said the woman, whose name was Francesca.

So they had the fried chicken and ate, enfolded by the calming susurrus of people talking, the tinkle of silverware. It was a nice restaurant, with leather seats and cloth napkins. "It's good to see you again," Julio said. "How are you doing?"

Francesca tried to peel through the many layers of that question.

"I'm okay," she said. "I think I'll still be able to see you for another week or so."

Julio nodded, his eyes sad, bottomless. "That's good," he said, and again, "That's good. You should take care of yourself." The pork skin crunched like glass in Francesca's mouth. "We should do something nice today."

"This is nice," Francesca said, smiling. Not a lot of things made her smile nowadays.

"We could go for a walk?" Julio said. "Or a movie? Or—"

Julio stopped talking. Francesca followed his gaze and saw a tall woman standing by their booth. She was wearing a white dress with a thin black belt, the sort of dress a woman would wear to a corporate function. Her hair was tied in a tight bun, her eyelids black with a severe slash of yellow eyeshadow. She looked at their faces and walked away without saying anything.

"Francesca," Julio said, his tone urgent. "Sit over here."

"What?" Francesca said.

"Sit over here," Julio said, but it was too late. The woman in the white dress was back, sliding next to Francesca. In her hands was a big mug of hot tea.

"It turns out I'm at the right table after all," she said, smiling at Julio. She turned to Francesca and offered her hand. "My name is C.C. Pleased to meet you."

Francesca shook her hand, but only out of reflex, her mind still trying to figure out what was happening.

"Did you see the coconut cake at the dessert section?" C.C. asked her. "It looks delicious. You should try it."

Francesca glanced at Julio, who looked petrified.

"We're in the middle of dinner," she said.

"I'm sure Julio wouldn't mind getting us a slice," C.C. said. She pressed something on the palm of her hand, and a bluish light twinkled in Julio's chest.

He touched the light, looking resigned. "I'll be right back," he said, and stood up.

They watched him leave and join the buffet line at the other end of the restaurant. Francesca never understood why they had to line up here, when they could easily have the food whisked to their table.

To her surprise, C.C. said, "It's part of the authentic experience." C.C. showed her the palm of her hand, which had five glowing letters: QUIET. The rest of the room took on a paler hue.

"Are you the Moderator?"

C.C. shook her head and showed her the logo of the All-Network on the palm of her hand, glowing like silver ink. "I'm the Community Guidelines Committee. C.C. for short."

"And?" Francesca said, though her heart started hammering inside her chest. "I don't have an eating disorder."

C.C. sighed. "I know," she said. "Walking to your table I already saw five Guests that I could kick out and ban right here and now." She gestured to a teenager across the aisle eating fish stew on top of a huge mound of steaming rice. "Before that girl entered this subNetwork, she posted her photo with a caption that read 'one like = one hour of fasting'. She's been in here for three days straight. That's a 72-hour fast. And she's got 90 likes and counting."

"She's going to die," Francesca said, without much emotion.

"But with the taste of fantastic fish stew lingering on her tongue!" C.C. said, smiling, mimicking the voice of the woman doing the VO in the All-Network ads. "She's a sad case, but she's not my case right now."

"Look," Francesca said. "We haven't broken any rules. You can check our logs. We only eat one meal a day here. Two, at most, and the second one only a small snack, like a bowl of porridge, or—"

"You're dying too, aren't you?"

That shocked her. Francesca decided that the only way to shut down this conversation was to feign ignorance. "What are you talking about?"

"You've been connected to the All-Network on and off for four days now," C.C. said. "So you escaped quarantine only to go into quarantine. Isn't that strange?"

Francesca said nothing.

"You know I can ban you from the All-Network."

"You can't—"

"Unless," C.C. said, holding up a finger. "Unless you tell me Julio's exact location."

Francesca massaged her arm, a nervous gesture. She looked away.

"I know you and Julio are not staying in the same place," C.C. said. "So if you tell me, you'll be safe and warm inside the All-Network until you expire. And you get seven days of Premium access for free, as per our Network rules. Don't you want a taste of Kobe beef, or caviar, or white truffle? Don't you want to go skydiving, or watch the entire Criterion Collection catalogue?" She smiled. "But if you don't give me his location, both you and Julio will be kicked out and banned." She took a sip of her tea. "The truth is, the Bureau of Quarantine wanted both of your locations, but the All-Network told them, either they get one location, or you both clam up and they get nothing. Better one location than nothing, right?"

In her head, Francesca examined that word—*expire*—as if it were a rare flower.

C.C. showed her her palm. On it are three silver digits, counting down from 300. "You have five minutes."

"What difference does it make?" Francesca said. "It will be over soon for Julio and me."

"What difference does it make?" C.C. echoed. "You have an airborne disease with a 67 percent case fatality rate in a densely populated city, and you ask me what difference it makes? It may be over soon for you and Julio, but what about for your neighbors? For everyone else?"

C.C. pressed her open palm on the table, and the table, beneath the plates of pork, chicken, salad and fruits, lit up with the dwindling digits.

"Why did you do it?" she said. "Why did you leave the hospital? You had a bed, and food, and medicine. People to take care of you."

Francesca left the moment the second test came back positive. The medical facility required two positive results, and patients were not supposed to leave until both results were released. Two positives meant mandatory quarantine. But the nurses were overwhelmed by the volume of people in the waiting rooms (she wondered where Julio was, at that moment still a stranger, when she decided to just get up and leave) and she, still a week or two away from hemorrhaging her internal organs, was able to slip out without anyone stopping her. She went back to her apartment, locked her door, arranged her remaining stock of food and water around her bed, and hooked up to the All-Network.

"I didn't want to die there."

"So you'd rather die *here* and wherever you are actually lying in bed right now, endangering the rest of the city while you wine and dine inside the All-Network."

"So I'm selfish," Francesca said. "So I'm only thinking of my own comfort. So what? Would you have done differently?" At least here I can still ingest solid food, Francesca thought. At least here the air doesn't smell like rot.

"Oh, I understand selfishness," C.C. said. "He reported you, you know."

Francesca turned to her, surprised.

"You're just saying that. You're just saying that so I'd turn on him."

"Why do you think he looked so frightened when he saw me? Yesterday he contacted me and said a patient has been lurking in this subNetwork for days with a masked IP address. The Quarantine Wards have no access to the All-Network, so we took it seriously. When I followed up with Julio, he gave me your name, but said he didn't know where you live. He said to give him time so he can try to find out."

The numbers on the table continued to count down.

"We figured," C.C. said, "that a patient would only confide in a fellow patient. Unless that patient is just stupid, and despite escaping quarantine, you don't really seem stupid to me, Francesca."

Francesca was quiet for several moments.

"When you report someone, you get seven days Premium access?" she said in a small voice.

"For free," C.C. said.

Do I even have seven days? Francesca thought. Am I only worth seven days? She felt her tears fall in two directions, down her cheeks in the restaurant, and down her temples in the stifling room where she lay dying, a pail full of bloody vomit next to her bed.

C.C. took Francesca's hand, her touch gentle. "You just met him here, didn't you?" C.C. said. "He's a stranger. You don't really know him." C.C. pressed Francesca's open palm on the tabletop, transferring the digits to Francesca's palm. "You have one minute."

When color came back to the room and Julio returned to their booth with a slice of coconut cake, he looked disoriented. "I don't know why I got this flavor," he said. "I don't even like coconut."

"I do," Francesca said.

"I wish I knew where you lived so I could visit you," Julio said, handing her a fork, and Francesca's hand trembled. "I mean *really* visit you, outside of the All-Network. I'm still strong enough to walk. Would you like me to visit you? Tell me where you live."

Francesca looked at his smile, at his eyes, and dropped her gaze to look at the number counting down on her palm: 10, 9, 8.

BLESSED ARE THOSE WHO SUFFER

Dearest,

In your last email you said you can still hear the sound of casement windows creaking open in a room that no longer has windows.

I'm glad you came to me with this, because now I can finally tell you this story.

(Yes, they are called "casement windows". I know all about windows, having read about them and having stared at them years and years after what happened. That room used to have "double casement windows" that swung in and out on side hinges. I know about "awning windows" and "sash windows" and "picture windows" and "double hung windows", and "meetings" and "muntins" and "drip caps" and "sills".)

This happened twenty-five years ago, before you were born, when your mother and I were still on speaking terms. I was seventeen and your Tito Jim was eighteen and we were home alone.

I can't remember now where everyone else was. Where your mother was. Perhaps they went to Manila. Or we were invited to see a relative I didn't like and I had a shouting match with Mama and your Tito Jim volunteered to stay with me. I was a *loud* teenager, what you'd call "difficult."

It was just six in the evening but it was as dark as midnight because of the storm. We were watching TV on the ground floor when we heard a loud bang coming from upstairs. We thought it was the wind hitting the windows, and already I imagined broken glass all over my bedroom floor, rainwater bursting into my room and drenching my bedsheets. We shot up from the sofa as though electrocuted and ran upstairs to see the damage. We had not turned on the lights at this point, so all we could see was the shape of *someone* or *something* trying to climb through the window. We could hear a squelch, a disgusting wet sound, like the sound of garbage that had decomposed and turned to mush. The room smelled as if it were filled with rotten food. A second after we turned on the light we screamed and slammed the door shut. It was only a second but we knew what we saw: long hair, a woman's face, gray limbs, black talons, bat wings—

My brother and I attempted to run out of the house, but the downpour was so strong and so loud that we couldn't even make ourselves step out the door. (But perhaps it was *her*, I thought. Perhaps she was not letting us leave.) We should call the Kapitan. We should call the barangay tanod. We should call Mama and Papa. We should call the priest. But this was before the time of texting and smartphones. The phone lines were down.

And even if we were able to contact someone, how will they leave their homes in this weather? We were both hysterical. Would she fit through the window? Is she in my room now? *Did we lock the door?*

Armed with knives from the kitchen, we went back to my room. My brother pressed his ear against the door. "Can you hear that?" he asked. We could hear a woman crying. We opened the door a little bit, and peeked. The creature's left wing was pinned against one-half of the double casement windows. Did the wind blow it shut? Did she injure her own wing with her panicked movements? The other half of the windows had swung in completely so it was flat against my bedroom wall. Her breasts swung as she kept herself in place, her left hand gripping the ledge. I couldn't see past her torso, but I knew below her waist there was nothing but intestines swinging in the wind. We could hear the furious flaps of her right wing, free but useless. Her right arm had a long deep gash, and she was bleeding profusely. If she let go—if her left arm grew tired, if she slid down—she would tear her left wing in half.

"Help me," she said. She sounded young. She turned to me, then to my brother. Her eyes were bloodshot from crying. We were still standing at the doorway, about ten feet away from her. We could feel the spray of rainwater coming through the open window. Her hair was drenched and lay heavy on her shoulders. "Help me, *please*," she said. Her left arm trembled.

"And if you attacked us?" I found myself saying. Your Tito Jim shushed me and told me to stop talking to her, that she was evil. The manananggal said she was brought by the storm, that the wind slammed her against the side of our house. She was not here to harm us; all she wanted was to go back home.

"You can't trick us," Kuya said.

The creature tried to use her right arm to steady herself, and she screamed in pain. It sounded like a deeper kind of pain. She sounded like our Tita Azon in the hospital lobby many years ago, when the doctor told her that her son didn't survive the bus crash. The sound unnerved me. "I did not ask to be like this," she said. My brother pulled me back and closed the door again.

We left her there for seven hours. We sat in the living room with the TV silent, listening to the blowing wind. We fell asleep, we woke up. We debated.

"If she were beautiful," I said, "if she had white wings, you would have helped her without a second thought."

"This is not a question of beauty," he said. "You know what that thing is!"

"But wasn't she human once?" I countered.

We both knew why we waited all those hours without doing anything. We were hoping—wishing—praying—that the exposure, the cold weather, the physical torture, would end her life. We wished her heart would just stop. We wished she would die, so we wouldn't be burdened with this decision.

"This is terrible," I said to my brother, and I began to cry. "We are terrible."

We went back upstairs at one in the morning, my brother holding my hand. We never held hands. We weren't particularly affectionate toward each other, but that moment I was so scared I was shaking, and he held my hand. When we opened the door, the creature looked feverish, delirious, her eyelids fluttering. She was singing, swaying. Her left wing already had dozens of tiny cuts in it, like a kite hacked by tree branches.

"I could just push her," my brother said, and the creature snapped out of her delirium and said, in a soft voice, "Oh, you came back." I was crying as though I were the one in pain. I let go of my brother's hand and stepped forward.

"Wait," he said, pulling me back. "Let me do it." He moved forward, one slow step by one slow step, until he was close enough to reach the window handle. The creature watched him, still crying. She didn't move. "Thank you," she said, and my brother cranked the window open to free her wing.

The searchers found his left slipper three miles away, in another town. Lodged in a santan bush as though it had fallen from a great height. (I took this slipper to my parents but they wouldn't believe it was his. It was a generic brand, they said. It could have been anyone's.) The storm passed the next day, morning came with bright sunlight, and I thought your mother and my parents would come home to find a trail of blood and entrails on the side of the house, where the creature who abducted your Tito Jim held onto the windowsill for seven hours, counting on our kindness.

But they saw *nothing*. There was nothing. No piece of skin from a bat wing, no broken talon. No smell. The storm blew it all away.

For years after what happened—the many painful years of searching for my brother—I would hear the sound of a window creaking open, even when all the windows in the room I was in were bolted shut. My parents had the wall of my bedroom torn down and rebuilt without the windows. The sound continued to haunt me, and so I left the room, the house. The town.

I know what your mother has been telling you. That Kuya just ran away, that I was not right in the head. That you shouldn't believe me.

I don't care if you believe me or not. All I want is for you to at least consider living somewhere else. All I want is for you to live your life without thinking that an act of compassion will one day destroy you.

Do you understand?

Yours with all my love,

PS Do you know the sound follows me even now? At one in the morning, without fail, wherever I am—I hear the sound of a window creaking open.

THE GHOSTS OF SINAGTALA

It was Good Friday. The penitents were out on the
street, flogging themselves, their backs covered in blood.
When the jeepney stalled, Emma leaned forward and
looked past the windshield. Four men, their faces covered
with maroon cloth topped with wreaths of bayabas leaves,
were lying facedown on the ground. Another man, in
cutoffs and a cap and holding a whip, hovered over them
and hit their buttocks with gusto. *Thwap. Thwap. Thwap.*
The man in cutoffs nudged them with his foot, and the
men rose and changed positions. The man in cutoffs
whacked them again. Emma could see the dust rising off
the penitents' shorts as the whip landed. Their bloodied
backs, glistening in the sun like oil, reminded Emma of
gutted fish.

The group changed positions two more times. The
penitents' heads faced north, east, west, south. They were
arranging their bodies in the form of a cross.

Inside the jeepney, the others passengers craned their
necks but quickly lost interest, save for one, a boy in a UP

shirt, who took out his phone and took a picture of the penitents. "It's been years since I last saw something like this," Ben said. One passenger wasn't patient enough to wait for the jeepney to start moving. Emma pulled their bags closer to her knees to let him pass.

"Are we going to ride another jeepney after this one?" she asked.

"No, just one more tricycle," Ben said. "Then we're home."

Home, Emma mused. The penitents stood up, genuflected, and took up their whips again. As they passed, the jeepney driver quickly drew the cloth serving as a window cover covering his side of the vehicle. The passengers followed suit and shut the windows. Emma wasn't quick enough. A penitent scourged his back, the whip falling, oddly with a sound like that of gravel dropping, and a drop of blood fell on her dress.

"Oh, no," Ben said. "Sorry, Em." He took out his handkerchief and dabbed at the stain near the neckline. Emma, embarrassed by this display of affection, pushed his hands away.

"It's all right, Kuya," she said. The jeepney started moving, and the siblings sat back and looked out the window.

"It always felt like this here during Lent," Ben said. Notes of pasyon drifted into the jeepney, the old woman's voice rising and falling like a wave. *Pagdaka'y ibubulalas parusang kasindak-sindak sa harap ng taong lahat.* "Like the town's hallucinating."

THE TRICYCLE DRIVERS were playing chess beneath the shade of a tree, sweating and sleepy in the late afternoon heat. Emma could feel her temper fraying. She wished her brother had rented a car. She tied her hair in a tight bun, hoping for a cool breeze to caress her nape.

"Where are you headed?" one of the tricycle drivers asked.

"Sinagtala," Ben said. When that didn't elicit a response, he added, "Del Estrella?"

The tricycle driver had a towel around his neck. He mopped his face with it as he looked at Ben, like he's trying to decide what to do with him. The driver stepped back and talked to his friends. They talked in low, urgent voices.

Another man stepped forward, younger and slighter than the first man who had spoken to them. "Let's go," he said, and helped them secure their luggage on top of the tricycle.

Emma marveled at how fast darkness fell in the town, cloaking the dirt roads at half-past five. Ben wanted to check his mail, but there was no mobile signal. He slid his phone back in his pocket. They passed by a sari-sari store selling halo-halo. They passed by a small house, white sheets on the clotheslines flapping in the wind. The road grew wider as the houses diminished in number. Trees on either side, their branches forming a roof over their heads. An impoverished cow feeding on the dying grass. The light was fading. At one point the tricycle driver made a wrong turn, and they ended up on an empty field.

"Are we lost?" Ben asked, apprehensive. "Let's ask someone." But there was no one to ask. The boy tried to find the road again, and did so after ten minutes that flowed like molasses.

"You're not going to leave us in the middle of nowhere, are you?" Ben said, and the boy laughed nervously.

He asked if they were relatives of the mansion's owner.

"We inherited it," Ben said.

The boy didn't ask them anything else after that.

When Emma was finally able to see Sinagtala through the trees, an imposing stone house with windows made of capiz shells, the boy stopped the tricycle and said that was as far as he could go.

Ben was instantly angry. "What do you mean? The roads are level here. Drop us off at least at the gate."

The boy wouldn't look him in the eye as he apologized.

"Unbelievable." He yanked the bags out of the boy's hands when they got off. "I should just pay you half the fare."

"Why won't you go closer to the house?" Emma asked.

She looked up the road. The house named after starlight was shrouded in darkness.

"It's not allowed," the boy said.

"Says who?" But the boy just revved his motor and drove away.

Ben had taken out his flashlight. "Sorry," he said, and drew Emma closer as they walked with their luggage, their strollers making a soft whir. Ben apologized as though everything were his fault. Perhaps it was.

The house was blazing with light. Was the house lit when Emma saw it through the trees? She couldn't remember.

"Well," Ben said, switching off his flashlight, "I can't wait to see the electric bill."

The gate was unlocked when they reached it. There was a folded note left between the bars.

"It's from the caretaker," Ben said. "It says here he doesn't stay after dark. Keys on the front porch. That's careless, isn't it? Leaves the gates unlocked, leaves the keys right out in the open."

"We don't have any neighbors," Emma said. "At least not nearby." *And the tricycle driver won't even come near the house.*

"Yes, but still." They stepped inside, and Ben locked the gate. They walked up the driveway and found a large set of bronze keys on the front porch, the keys all tied with a red ribbon. He picked them up. "Come on."

Ben tried several keys before he was finally able to open the double doors. When he did, the siblings were hit with a blast of cold wind, a breeze imprisoned within the stone walls now finally set free. Emma expected to see a grand staircase, chandeliers, vases of flowers, but the ground floor was bare and had a low ceiling.

"Well, that's disappointing," Emma said.

Ben turned to her and smiled. "It's an old house. In most mansions during the Spanish era, the lower floor serves as the stables. The living rooms are upstairs."

There was a staircase straight ahead. Ben climbed it first, helping Emma with her bags. "Here we go," Ben said, when they emerged onto the second floor. They found themselves in the sala. The plump sofa and chairs were white and gold, the curtains cream. Emma finally got her flowers and her chandeliers. Gilt mirrors hung on the walls, along with portraits of the siblings' ancestors and Sinagtala's original owners framed in dark wood. Felix and Ernestina del Estrella looked out of one painting, watching the siblings with expressionless eyes. Emma looked away.

There were bowls of sampaguita blossoms on every table, and the room smelled sweet and bright.

"It's beautiful," Emma said. She went behind the sofa, which was facing the staircase, and pushed open the capiz windows. Acres of trees, then the gleam of the river. Emma felt the cool breeze on her face and neck, and closed her eyes.

She heard the flick of a lighter. "Kuya!" she said, opening her eyes and turning to him. Ben took a long drag on his cigarette and blew the smoke out of the side of his mouth. He looked sheepish.

"Sorry," Ben said. "Just one cigarette?"

"But you'll make the house smell like you," she said, frowning.

"Just one cigarette," Ben said. Emma sighed and let him be.

"When you were with Megan you stopped smoking," she said, and she stopped thinking of the cigarette and started thinking about Megan. Megan and her brother broke up just before this trip. "You never told me what happened. I thought you two were going to get married."

Ben shrugged. "It just didn't work out."

They stood together in silence for a while, looking at the dark trees.

"How old is this house?" Emma asked.

"Around two hundred years?" Ben said. "It has always been known as Del Estrella. 'Of the star.' I think it's our great-grandfather who changed the name to Sinagtala, 'Starlight.'" He laughed. "In a sudden fit of Tagalog pride."

"Have I been here before?"

"Once. I was eleven and you were a baby." Ben smiled around his cigarette. "I've been here maybe five or six times. Summer vacations, to see our grandparents. Father's parents. The first time you were brought here was the last time we came here. Fifteen years ago. Just before Father died. Then our grandparents moved out as well."

The Del Estrellas didn't like their mother very much. They only got in touch when she died six years ago—Ben twenty years old and Emma nine, suddenly orphans— and then stopped visiting after the funeral, making their existence known only through the occasional signed check and phone call. Their grandmother died a year ago and their grandfather mere months after that. That was when Ben got the papers and decided on taking this trip. It was summer, school was out, and he wanted to show Emma the ancestral home before she moved on to college.

"So no one's lived here for fifteen years?" Emma said. "Must be hell to clean."

"The caretaker oversees its cleaning every few months or so. I guess that makes up for his leaving the house wide open." Ben was planning to just flick the cigarette out the window but changed his mind, the sight of the trees stopping him. "Let's go get something to eat."

The kitchen was located to the left of the sala, past the huge dining room. They turned off some lights as they went. The charcoal stoves were still in place, but there was also a modern stove, an oven, a microwave, a toaster, and a refrigerator. It was startling to see modern appliances in a kitchen that looked so old. Ben put out his cigarette in the sink and checked the cupboards. Emma opened the refrigerator and peered in.

"Well, we're well-stocked," Ben said.

"We have meat," Emma announced.

"I'm too tired to cook," Ben said. "Can we just open up some cans?"

Ben opened a can of pork and beans and a can of sausages and dumped them in two bowls. The bowls were bone-white. He took a loaf of bread from the cupboard and stepped into the dining room.

The dining table could seat twenty people. There were cloth fans hanging from the ceiling, which could be moved by hand to shoo away flies. They sat in one corner, with Ben at the kabisera, the head of the table, and began to eat.

"What?" Ben said out of the blue halfway through their meal.

Emma looked up and frowned at her brother.

"Sorry," he said. "I thought you said something."

"I was just eating."

"Sorry."

"What time is it?" Emma asked. "I can't wait to take a shower."

"It's just past six."

"So early," Emma said. "It's so quiet here. Do you think they have a TV?"

"I don't think so." Ben took out his phone and turned on his media player. A pop song started playing, then stopped.

"Did your phone die?" Emma said.

"No." But it was dead when he checked. He glanced at the doorway. Something white drifted into the sala.

The lights went out.

"Oh, no," Emma said. "Tell me this house has a backup generator."

"It's okay," Ben said. He flicked open his lighter. In the glow of the tiny flame he saw Emma yawn and rub her eyes. Ben stood up and let her hold his left arm.

"Come on, sleepyhead," he said, walking to the doorway, the furniture barely visible in the darkness of the sala. The flame only threw a small circle of light in front of them. Emma's arms were wrapped around his, her dress swishing against his legs. "See how a smoker saves the day?"

"Where are you going?" Emma said in a plaintive voice. Ben turned around in shock.

Emma was still sitting on her chair.

"Well, don't leave me here," she said. "I'll get lost."

The pressure on his arm disappeared. The lights went back on in a blinding flash.

"Jesus," Ben muttered under his breath.

Emma yawned and rubbed her eyes, and Ben felt a chill.

"Let's get out of here," he said.

"But the dishes—"

"I'll wash them in the morning. Come on. Let's get settled."

THEY CROSSED THE sala to get to the rooms. There were two doors facing each other. Ben opened one. Inside was a simple king-size bed with a mattress and white sheets. On each side of the bed was a nightstand, each carrying a bronze angel figurine.

"I've never seen this room before," Ben said. He closed the door and opened the one facing it. Another king-size bed, but a four-poster this time, with an ornate headboard and curved legs. Near the windows, flush by the wall, was a table with a lamp.

"Here we go," Ben said.

"There are two master bedrooms?"

"That one must be the guest room. I'll show you something." He went behind the headboard and drew back a lace curtain that Emma had at first thought was wallpaper. Behind the curtain was a door.

"Oh," Emma said, delighted. They went through the door and saw themselves in another room, but with a queen-size bed this time.

"The girls' room," Ben said. There was a walk-in closet and another connecting door to another room.

In this room were two beds and a pair of study desks. "The boys' room," Ben said. Emma stood in the doorway that connected the rooms and looked from one side to the other.

"How come only the boys' room has study desks?" she asked.

"Well, it was the Spanish era, and only boys—"

"Goddamn misogynists," Emma said, and Ben burst out laughing.

"So I guess you'll take the master bedroom?" Emma said. She squatted with a grunt and zipped open her luggage by the queen-size bed.

"Yes," he said. "Each room has its own bath. I'll head out now and fix my things."

"Wait."

Ben turned back. Emma was clutching her towel and pajamas to her chest.

"Can you," Emma said, "can you wait outside the bathroom while I shower?"

"Oh," Ben said. "Okay. Sure. Let me grab a chair."

Emma left the bathroom door ajar. Ben sat outside, his back to the wall. "This house is so big," Emma said. "It's scaring me a little bit."

"You won't spend an hour showering, will you?" Ben said.

Emma was indignant. "I don't take that long!"

Ben chuckled. Every now and then, while showering, Emma would ask, "Are you still there?" and Ben would say, "Yes, I'm still here, Emma."

She was bathed and dressed after twenty minutes, her hair dripping with water. Ben was quick to note that Emma donned her pajamas inside the bathroom instead of using the dressing room, with its dividers and its many mirrors.

Emma held up the dress that was stained with blood earlier. "I was going to put this in a basin of water, but I can't find the detergent."

"It's in the laundry room, past the kitchen," Ben said, rubbing the cloth between his fingers. "It's okay. I'll take care of the laundry tomorrow."

Emma folded the dress and placed it on top of her luggage.

"All set?" Ben said. "Good night."

"I can keep you company, too, if you want."

Ben smiled. "I think I'll be okay, Em."

"I'll do it anyway. I brought a book."

After Ben finished taking a shower, he asked, gently, "Emma? Do you want to sleep here? We could share the bed."

"No, it's okay," Emma said, closing her book, suddenly embarrassed. "Good night." And they went to their separate bedrooms and turned off the lights.

BEN WAS ABLE to sleep right away out of sheer exhaustion, but two hours later he was wide-awake. He sat up, still groggy, and realized what was wrong.

His bedroom light was on.

Did he leave it on? He debated with himself whether he should get up and turn off the light, and decided to just leave it and try to go back to sleep. He couldn't. After nearly an hour of tossing and turning, he took out a book and tried not to think of the stories his relatives and his grandparents' househelp had told him about this house, stories that his own grandparents branded as nonsense.

"We've lived here for years and we never felt anything out of the ordinary," his grandfather used to say, though why did they move out after so many years? Why did they suddenly abandon Sinagtala?

In the other room, Emma, half-asleep, heard something rustling at the foot of her bed. She bolted upright, wide-eyed in the darkness, and heard a boy's voice say, very clearly, "It's going to be all right."

Emma jumped out of the bed and ran to the master bedroom.

Ben looked up from his book. "Em?" he said. "Can't sleep?"

"I heard something," Emma said, then crawled under the sheets and fell asleep beside her brother.

AT THREE IN the morning, Ben, who had just fallen asleep, was awakened by the sound of Emma giggling.

"O?" Ben said, amused. "You're dreaming."

"Where are they?" Emma said.

"Who?"

Emma giggled. "Where are they?"

"Who, Em?'

"Felicia and Tomas!" she said, happily, and fell asleep again.

SATURDAY CAME. THE morning light washed away the shadows and the unsettling fears of the night before. Ben, singing softly, washed last night's dishes and prepared breakfast. A proper one. Garlic rice and eggs and tuyo and coffee. Emma ate everything and marveled at how clear the sky was. She tied her hair, grabbed her phone, and announced that she wanted to go exploring.

Sinagtala only had two stories, but it was very wide, expanding from the sala to either side with all its rooms and connecting doors. "I wasn't able to show you this last night," Ben said, and opened a door that led from the sala to the azotea. In the middle of the terrace was a fountain, no longer working. There was bougainvillea all around, white and red and dark pink, as well as bushes of sampaguita and wild rose, and pots of cadena de amor and dama de noche. Emma demanded that Ben take a picture of her posing by the fountain and the flowers, scrutinizing each shot to see if they could be used as an Instagram profile pic. They found a pair of watering cans in a corner, and proceeded to water the garden.

"What do you plan to do with the house?" Emma asked. "Are you going to sell it?"

"I haven't thought about it," Ben said.

"Call Megan. Maybe she'll agree to marry you once she finds out that you now own a mansion."

Ben didn't answer.

"Sorry," Emma said. "I liked her, you know."

"I know," Ben said. "Let's get going?"

There was a hallway beyond the boys' room that remained dark despite the bright morning. From there they entered a room that served as an entertainment den for guests but looked more like a museum. There were photographs of various sizes in various degrees of fading on the walls. Coffee-colored doñas in baro't saya sat stiffly on chairs, large cuts of diamonds on their throats and earlobes. Men in amerikana stood with canes, hand on their lapel or tucked into their coats. There was a photo of a young girl, around four years old, lounging on a sofa with strings of pearls around her neck.

Inside the room, a piano sat darkly in a corner while a chess set made of yakal brooded between two tables.

Ben knelt to peer at the chess set. "Look at this, Em," he said, picking up a pawn. "Mahogany. You can still smell the wood."

But Emma was preoccupied with another photograph, smaller than the others. It was a photograph of a young couple. The woman wasn't looking at the camera. "Eighteen ninety-nine," Emma read the inscription. "Felicia and Tomas. You've heard of them?" Emma asked, noticing the look on Ben's face.

Ben, suddenly mute, shook his head.

"She looks too young to be his wife," Emma said.

"May-December love affair," Ben said, looking elsewhere.

They moved on. They peeked into the chapel ("They have their own chapel?" Emma said, impressed) and finally arrived at the library.

Books filled the shelves from floor to ceiling. There were some books in glass cases: the Old Testament, a copy of *Noli* and *Fili*, an edition of *Florante at Laura*.

Emma peeked at the titles. "If you do sell the house," she said, "let's keep all of the books."

Ben laughed. "Deal." He spotted a pile of books in the deepest corner of the library. He sat down, sneezing at the dust, and picked one book, a thin volume bound in sheepskin.

It was a series of ink sketches. On the first page, a beautiful young woman with chains of dama de noche in her hair. *Enero, 1899.* Ben smiled.

His smile faded when he turned the page. *Marso, 1899.* It was the same sketch, but the young woman now wore thorns instead of flowers.

The sketch was transforming. *Abril, 1899,* black holes for eyes. *Mayo, 1899,* a black hole for a mouth, the young woman clutching the thorns and screaming in agony. *Hunyo, 1899,* the young woman, with claws for arms, rips the thorns apart, as well as the top of her head. *Hulyo, 1899,* the soft lines of the sketch disappear and were replaced with geometric shapes, the young woman reduced to triangles and squares. Triangle eyes, triangle mouth, square head. Little triangles and squares in her hair. The shapes were drawn on top of each other and looked like they were vibrating. Moving.

It was the last sketch.

Ben threw the book away with a shiver and picked up another one.

Mahal kong Tomas,
May daga sa ilalim ng ating kama may daga
sa ilalim ng ating kama may daga sa ilalim ng
ating kama may daga sa ilalim ng ating kama
may daga sa ilalim ng ating kama may daga

My beloved Tomas. There's a rat under our bed there's a rat under our bed there's a rat under our bed. Over and over. For one hundred and fifty pages. Ben threw the book back on the pile as well and stood up.

"That's creepy," Emma said, who had been looking over his shoulder.

"What's that?"

Emma was carrying a thick leather-bound volume. "It's filled with old newspaper clippings," she said. "Looks interesting."

They walked back to the sala, but Ben stopped by the guest room. "I want to check something," he said. Inside the room were two doors. One led to the bathroom. The other was yet another connecting door. "Ah," Ben said, and walked through.

They stopped dead in their tracks. The room was empty, save for a painting that completely covered one wall. It was Henry Fuseli's *The Nightmare*, with its white-eyed horse, its demon sitting on the maiden's chest.

"What the fuck," Ben said.

"That's horrible," Emma said, shrinking away from the painting. "What is this room for?"

"I don't know," Ben said. "Let's get out of here."

Ben locked the door on their way out, and realized that the door locked only from the outside.

EMMA COOKED LUNCH this time. Pork sinigang, which Ben praised to high heavens. He then gathered up all their laundry in a large rattan basket they found in the kitchen ("How quaint," Emma commented) and headed to the laundry room.

"Wow," Emma said as she followed, looking around at the laundry room's white walls and white tiles. "It's like stepping into the future."

"It's a remodeled room." Ben placed the basket on the floor and started sorting the few pieces of clothing.

"You know we could just wait till our last day here before doing the laundry." They had planned to stay for seven days.

"I didn't bring a lot of clothes," Ben said.

"Ugh."

"You brought that with you?"

"Light reading," Emma said, and sank into a chair with the tome she got from the library open on her lap. "It's not just newspaper clippings, apparently. It's newspaper clippings about the family."

"Oh?" Ben put Emma's stained dress under the tap and applied a paste of laundry detergent on the stain.

"Yes, there's even a family tree in front. Nice lettering." Emma turned the pages, the paper sounding crisp and brittle. "Felicia and Tomas. They're the last entry here. Felicia's ten years younger."

"Good on you, Tomas," Ben said, and Emma looked at him and wrinkled her nose.

"Felicia del Estrella. Daughter of Arturo and Elvira. Born 1884."

"Arturo is Grandfather's grandfather," Ben said. "Felicia's our great-aunt."

Emma was quiet for a moment. "Felicia and Tomas died in the same year," she said. "Eighteen ninety-nine. They were just 15 and 25. Fifteen's too young to get married, don't you think?"

Ben shrugged. "Not in those days, I guess," he said, and looked at Emma. "Fifteen's too young to die."

"Wait," Emma said. "There's supposed to be a symbol on the chart when you're married. This wriggly thing." She turned back a page. "Oh my God."

"What?"

"They're not married," Emma said. "They're brother and sister."

Silence.

"They're our age," Emma said. "What's wrong?"

Ben was scrutinizing Emma's dress. The drop of blood still looked fresh. "This is one persistent stain," he said.

BEN WANTED TO catch up on sleep. Emma got to the master bedroom first. She noticed that the door to the guest room was wide-open. Emma stood in front of it, wondering. Beyond the doorway, she could see that the door to the strange room with the strange painting was also wide-open, the room that in her head she had called "the Nightmare room", the room that Ben had already locked that morning.

There was a girl inside the room. A girl in a black dress, sitting on the floor with her back to the door, her face on her knees, her arms around her head. The painting loomed over her, as large and as menacing as a full moon. "Stop," the girl said into her knees, and Emma thought, *How come I can hear her so clearly?* "Stop," the girl said, rocking back and forth. She was crying. "Stop. Stop. Stop."

Emma willed herself to move and run into the master bedroom.

MEGAN CAME TO Sinagtala. When Ben opened the front door, she was standing on the porch, carrying a bouquet of wild roses and dama de noche. It was early evening but the lights outside the house shone as bright as the sun.

"Megan?" he said. "What are you doing here?"

"I'm dropping by for a visit," she said, smiling.

"How did you know we were staying here?" He had never mentioned Sinagtala to her. He never had the chance to.

"Emma called me."

"Emma called you?"

"I want to try again," Megan said. "Maybe we can work something out."

Ben stared at her.

"Won't you let me in?"

"You're not real," Ben said.

Megan's smile faltered. The lights died, and Megan's face was shrouded in shadow.

Ben stepped away from the door. He could only see Megan's silhouette. The shape of her hair, the flowers in her arms.

"What do you mean I'm not real," the shadow said.

Ben woke up in the bedroom, alone.

"I CAN'T SLEEP!" Emma announced when Ben found her in the dining room, spreading peanut butter on a slice of bread. "And I got hungry. Want some?"

"Is that coffee?" Ben asked. Emma slid the cup to him.

Emma had opened the windows in the dining room. The sky looked pale. The room was filled with a soft, yellow light. Ben looked at his sister and almost said, *You look like someone from those old coffee-colored pictures.*

His hand shook as he placed the cup back on the saucer.

"Are you okay?" Emma said.

"Bad dream," said Ben.

"Sandwich?"

"What time is it?"

"Five?" Emma said. "It gets dark early here."

"I slept that long?"

"Remember when you overslept and Megan cooked us dinner?" Emma said. The back of Ben's neck stiffened. "You two were supposed to go on a date, but she decided to come over and cook pasta."

"Emma—"

"Did she cheat on you? Is that it?"

Ben slammed his open palm on the table, making the saucers jump.

"Ben?"

"She wanted you gone!" Ben said, suddenly filled with an inexplicable anger. "All right? She never liked you. She said we couldn't get married if you're still living with me. She said how could I even *think* of having a child with her if I'm still raising a child. There. Are you happy now?"

Emma, who was still holding the peanut butter-smeared bread knife in one hand and her sandwich in the other, looked shell-shocked.

"Emma?" said Ben, surprised and horrified by what he had said. "Emma, I'm sorry, I don't know what came over me—"

Emma stood up and walked around the table, giving him a wide berth. Ben reached out his hands to her. "Emma," Ben said. "Come on. I'm sorry. I didn't mean it."

Emma slammed the dining room door.

BEN RAN AFTER her and found her enter the guest room. "Em!" he called. Emma kept walking and went into the room with the painting.

She stood in the middle of the room, staring at the painting.

"Emma, what are you doing?"

Emma whirled around. She looked confused. "Kuya?" she said.

The door slammed in Ben's face.

"Kuya?" Emma said from behind the door. Ben tried the knob. The knob wouldn't turn.

"Em?"

"Kuya?"

"Emma, let go of the doorknob."

"Kuya? Kuya?"

Emma's voice was rising in panic.

"Kuya?" Emma banged on the door."Kuya, there's somebody in here! Kuya!"

"Damn it!" Ben exclaimed. "Emma?"

Emma started to scream.

"Emma!" Ben shouted, feeling as though the ground had opened up and swallowed him whole. He started to cry. Emma was screaming like a person slowly being burned alive.

Something large hit the door, and the room fell silent.

"Emma?" Ben tried the knob again. The knob turned.

"Emma!" Ben shouted, but the room was empty. Only the painting, secure in its silence, was able to hear him.

EMMA WAS IN the girls' bedroom, lying on her side, crying. She heard someone moving in the master bedroom. Ben. He knocked on the connecting door. "Are you there?" he said.

"Don't come in here!" Emma said. "Go away!"

"I'm sorry."

Emma stood up and sat by the door, leaning her head against it. "You're not sorry. You're wishing what you've wished every day since I was nine: that I just died with Mother."

"Don't say that. Don't ever say that."

"You were twenty when she died. You could have lived on your own. Saved more money. Settled down. But I'm still here, holding you back."

"Emma?"

Emma looked up. Her brother was standing next to her.

"Oh my God, you're all right!" Ben said. Ben's eyes were wet. "Who were you talking to?"

Emma looked at Ben, at the connecting door, then back at Ben. "I was talking to you."

Ben shook his head. "I wasn't in the master bedroom. I got locked out. None of the keys worked. I was hoping to get in through here." He knelt next to her. "Oh God, I'm glad you're all right."

Emma stood up and wrenched open the connecting door. The master bedroom was empty.

"Emma," Ben said, "about what I said earlier—"

Emma walked out of the room. Ben followed close behind, not daring to take his eyes off her. She ran through the sala, stopped when she reached the azotea, and sat suddenly on the ground near the flowers, as though the strength had left her legs.

"I'm really sorry," Ben said, standing by the fountain. He didn't know what else to say.

"When we get back," Emma said, "I'll start looking for a place to rent."

"Emma—"

"I'll start looking for a place to rent," Emma insisted. "I'm going to college anyway. I'll find a cheap studio apartment near the campus. I can use the money Grandfather left us to pay for the deposit and the advance and the furniture and appliances, then I can, I don't know, then I can get a *job*." Emma was doing something to the flowers but Ben couldn't see. "Tutoring. Writing papers. I don't know. I'll figure it out."

"Emma," Ben said. "You don't have to do that."

"You can stop supporting me," Emma said. "You'll finally be free to do whatever you want. You can go abroad. You can get married." Ben covered his face. "You can marry Megan."

She stood up and brushed past him. "You can call that cold-hearted bitch and ask her to spend a weekend here," she said as she walked back inside. "I hope the house chokes her to death!"

The sun was starting to set. The azotea looked like it was burning. Ben looked at the ground and saw with a shock what his sister had made—a chain of dama de noche.

EMMA DIDN'T WANT to eat dinner. She also didn't want to sleep in any of the rooms, so Ben brought out some pillows and a blanket to the sala, which she accepted without a word.

While Emma got settled on the sofa, Ben went to the kitchen and put the food back in the refrigerator. He was standing at the sink when he noticed someone peeking at him from the kitchen doorway. "Emma?" he said, even though he knew it wasn't Emma. The figure walked away. Ben hurried back to the sala. Emma pulled up her blanket and tried to get comfortable. Ben sat on one of the chairs, wondering how he'd be able to go to sleep.

Emma woke up in the middle of the night coughing and choking. When she got her breath back, she realized that she was sitting on the floor inside the guest room, holding one of the bronze angel figurines. She was wearing the dress she wore when she got to Sinagtala, the one with the blood drop, the one with the stain that Ben couldn't remove.

What am I doing here? she wondered, looking at the blood drop, and watched in horror as the blood drop multiplied—

Emma felt a warm spray on her face. Her hands were wet and sticky. In her right hand, the angel figurine felt as heavy as the world.

The figurine was covered in blood.

Her fingers were covered in blood.

On the floor in front of her lay her brother, his skull cracked open. Blood flowed out of the wound in a regular pulse.

BEN WAS SITTING on a chair when Emma woke up screaming on the sofa. He was watching her.

"Bad dream?" Ben felt sad, sadder than he had ever been. "Let's get you to bed."

"I don't want to," Emma said, but her voice was feeble, her muscles weak. Ben led her to the guest room and helped her lie down.

"I don't want to be here," Emma said. Ben smoothed back her hair. He was leaning so close he could smell soap on Emma's skin.

"I know," Ben said, and took a pillow and covered her face with it.

Emma thrashed wildly. Ben lifted his knee and lowered it on his sister's chest, his arms straining to keep the pillow in place. He was thinking, *Emma would never be able to live on her own. She wouldn't get a job, or if she did, she wouldn't be able to keep it long enough to make rent. She'd go back, in the end, she'd go back even before I could live my own life.* He cried. His sobs grew louder as his sister's limbs grew weaker. He screamed when Emma stopped moving. His scream echoed around the dark room.

He removed the pillow, placed it by Emma's side, and stood up, turning away. From behind him came a loud gasp, then violent coughing, the rustle of cloth.

He turned back. Emma was sitting up, clutching the nightstand. He couldn't believe his eyes. "Emma—"

"You tried to kill me," Emma said, her voice hoarse, her eyes bloodshot.

Emma lifted the angel figurine and hit him across the face, spraying herself with his blood.

BEN WOKE UP wheezing and found himself on the bed inside the guest room. He clutched the nightstand and felt his fingers touch the base of the angel figurine sitting there. He cried out. "No," he said. "No. No." He cried into his hands.

Emma appeared by the door, wearing her pajamas. "Kuya?" she said, cautious. "What are you doing here?"

Am I awake now? Ben wanted to ask.

"Am I awake now?" Emma asked, making Ben shiver.

Emma switched on the light. Ben reached out to her, and Emma embraced him.

WHEN EMMA FELL asleep again on the sofa, Ben took out the leather-bound book and leafed through it. His eyes ached. His tongue itched for a cigarette. On one page was a photo of Tomas with a curly-haired woman, flashing a smile at the camera. *March, 1899. Tomas del Estrella & Amanda Pelaez.*

The sky was already turning pink when Ben was able to piece together a story from the photos and news clippings. At around five in the morning, Ben found a folded letter between the pages, yellowed with age.

The letter was written in an almost undecipherable scrawl:

Mahal kong Daga,
May Tomas sa ilalim ng ating kama may Tomas
sa ilalim ng ating kama may Tomas sa ilalim
ng ating kama may Tomas sa ilalim ng ating
kama may Tomas sa ilalim ng ating kama

My beloved Rat. There's a Tomas under our bed there's a Tomas under our bed there's a Tomas under our bed—

"Oh my God," Ben said. The book fell to the floor with a thud.

Emma sat up. "What's happening?"

"We need to get out of here," Ben said.

AS THEY HAULED out their luggage, folded their clothes and put on their shoes, Ben told her the story. He spoke in a soft voice, as though afraid someone else might hear.

"Felicia was sick," Ben said. "Very sick. Maybe early-onset schizophrenia, but the term 'schizophrenia' didn't even exist then. Her parents kept her cooped up in here instead of sending her to an asylum. When they passed away in 1898, her brother, Tomas, was the only one left to take care of her. What we called the guest room was their room."

Emma stopped folding and looked at him.

"The room with the painting was where Tomas locked her whenever she turned," Ben bit the inside of his cheek, "violent."

"But that painting!" Emma said. "How does he think that will help—"

"The painting was her choice," Ben said. "At least according to the written accounts."

Emma shook her head.

"In March 1899, Tomas got engaged to a woman named Amanda. It was then that Tomas realized that he couldn't be married and take care of Emma at the same time."

"'Emma'?" Emma said.

"What?"

"Did you say 'Emma'?"

Ben thought for a moment. "I said Felicia."

Emma took a deep breath. "Go on."

"Tomas decided to send Felicia to a mental asylum in Barcelona," Ben said. "Relatives would help him with the transfer. Felicia found out, somehow, and became very hysterical and hostile. There was an account of her running out of the mansion and attacking a little girl on the street.

"One night, while she was sleeping, Tomas took a pillow and—"

Ben's breath caught in his throat. He sat down on the sofa. "He took a pillow and smothered his sister in her sleep."

"Felicia died?" Emma said, sitting down as well.

Ben shook his head. "Not at that moment. When Tomas thought she was dead, he turned away, but Felicia was still alive then. She took one of the angel figurines and hit him."

Silence. Emma looked around the house with wary eyes.

"But of course it's all speculation," Ben said. "Police conjectures and so on. They're not exactly CSI."

Both of them decided not to mention their dreams.

"And Felicia?" Emma said. "What happened to her?"

"They found her body on the driveway," Ben said. "She was covered in her brother's blood, but she had no wounds. They don't know how she died."

"Poor Felicia," Emma said. "Poor Tomas."

They resumed packing.

"Emma," Ben said.

Emma looked up.

"I don't mind not getting married," Ben said. "I don't mind not having a family. I want to see you grow old. I don't mind if I end up in a house alone with just a pair of dogs and a bunch of cats, as long as you're happy." He was quick to amend himself. "But I'll live in a small house. Not this house." Ben looked up at the ceiling. "This house is too big."

They were quiet for several moments. Emma leaned forward and gave him a small peck on the cheek, something she had not done since she turned twelve and became self-conscious.

Ben smiled and grabbed their bags. "Let's get out of here."

DARKNESS FELL SWIFTLY outside Sinagtala. Inside, Ben flicked on lights as they walked across the sala and down the stairs to the empty stables. "Stay beside me, Emma," Ben said, carrying a bag in each hand. There was the door, there was the open road, bathed in blue and violet. Emma was standing right beside her brother when the lights died.

The next thing she knew, Ben was standing on the front porch and she was still inside the house. "Emma?" Ben said, confused, stepping forward to reach her, but the double doors slammed shut between them.

There were windows in the lower floor but for some reason Emma found herself in complete darkness. "Kuya!" she screamed repeatedly. Ben was banging on the door on the other side.

Suddenly he stopped. A suffocating silence fell.

"Kuya?" Emma said. She whirled around to face the stairs. She couldn't see. She walked slowly, arms outstretched in front of her, praying fervently that her hands wouldn't touch someone standing in the way.

If the lower floor was inexplicably dark, the upper floor was unusually bright, the sala dazzling, the chandelier as brilliant as a teardrop. She had to find another way out of Sinagtala, but she felt rooted to the spot.

"Emma!" Ben zoomed out of the dining room and practically tackled her.

Emma was relieved, overjoyed. She clutched his arms. "How did you get in?"

Ben smiled down at her. "The kitchen," he said. But he led her away from it.

"Kuya? Where are we—"

Ben was taking her to the guest room.

"No." Emma struggled to get out of his grip. She thrust out her hands to grab at a lamp, a table edge, the wall, anything to keep them from moving. "No! No!"

Ben lifted her up from the ground. Emma felt one of her nails break, felt her head fill with heat. They barged through the bedroom door and Ben threw her on the bed. *You're not Ben*, she thought. *You're not real.* She cried, knowing what was coming. The pillow fell on her face like a block of cement. *He will put his knee on my chest*, Emma thought in the face of that approaching darkness.

Emma struggled with all her might, kicking and clawing. Ben fell to the floor, still holding the pillow. "You're not real!" Emma screamed. She swiped the angel figurine from the nightstand and hit him across the face. Pretend-Ben fell back, a large gash appearing on his cheek, his mouth filling with a wet sound. "You're not real," Emma whispered, feeling the warm blood splash on her face and chest, and hit him again. And again. And again.

Pretend-Ben stopped moving. He lay there with his eyes open, his lips parted. Emma, crying, pushed him under the bed. *My beloved Rat. There's a Tomas under our bed there's a Tomas under our bed there's a Tomas under our bed.*

"Stop!" Emma pleaded. "Please, just stop!" There was blood everywhere. She leaned her head against the mattress and saw her arms leave red streaks on the white cloth. She remembered the penitents, their backs slick like gutted fish.

"You're not real!" Emma said, but the blood felt and smelled real. The Nightmare room's door swung open, and the painting looked at her accusingly.

Ben's hand shot out from under the bed and grabbed her ankle.

Emma screamed and kicked him away. She ran—out of the hallway, past the sala, and down the stairs, where she almost fell. She hit the double doors with her shoulder and they swung right out, the night air chilling her skin. She kept running. In the middle of the driveway she fell to her knees and looked at her hands, her arms, her dress. The blood was still there.

Emma screamed. The trees and the sky and the stars and the daunting hulk of Sinagtala looked on, impassive, unmoved by her remorse.

Hours passed. Emma sat on the driveway hugging her knees. She rocked back and forth. She started to hum a song, forgot the melody she was humming, stopped, started again. Her brother's blood dried on her skin and fell away in flakes like petals. *I will die here,* she thought. *I will die here like this.*

"Emma?"

Ben—*Pretend-Ben?*—knelt in front of her, and Emma, whimpering, crawled away. Ben grabbed her from behind and held her close.

"Emma," Ben said. "Emma! It's me. I couldn't find a way into the house. I've been circling the mansion for half an hour when I saw you run out."

Emma stopped struggling. *Half an hour?*

She looked down at herself. Her arms and dress were clean.

"It's me," Ben said again.

Emma placed a hand on her brother's chest. He had no wounds. "Kuya," she said, cautiously, like a child learning a new word. She sobbed in his arms, her chest heaving.

"It's all right," Ben said, and helped her up. "We're all right." They walked down the driveway and out of the gates of Sinagtala to the roads beyond, and did not look back.

FAIRY TALES

There was a girl in a white dress crying inside the
MRT station. She was sitting all by herself on a bench
on the platform, farthest from the entrance but closest to
the doors of the first train car. She was all alone because
the train had just left, taking the rest of the commuters
with it. Dante, on his way to work, had missed the train.
He would have missed seeing the girl's wings, too, if he
weren't standing at the right angle.

The platform was again slowly filling up with new
passengers. Dante walked up to her, then stopped short.
He wondered how long she had been sitting there, how
many had seen her wings. Maybe no one had, Dante
thought, because if someone did, the guards would have
had picked her up and escorted her out of the station
before anyone could snap a picture. Fairies were prohibited
from displaying their wings in public.

So young. Perhaps less than two hundred moons.
Her wings were still transparent, still lacking that pink,
green, or lilac hue that Diwata wings take on with age. A

protester? But protesters didn't protest alone, unless there was a new movement for tearful, solitary demonstrations that Dante had failed to pick up from the evening news.

"Um," he said, finally finding the courage to speak to her. "I'm sorry, but I think you need to fold your wings now."

The girl looked up. Her expression nearly broke Dante's heart. "I can't," she said, hiccupping.

"You can't?"

"I can't," she repeated in a plaintive voice. "They wouldn't fold."

"How come?" Dante was confused. "Oh my goodness, are you injured?"

The girl cried. Dante glanced around and zoomed in on a guard facing their direction.

"You really need to cover yourself up," Dante said. "You might end up in jail. Can I put my jacket over your back?"

The girl nodded. Dante wore a jacket that was too big for him—Crystal often said he looked like a child in it— but it was successful in covering the girl's unmentionables.

"Is everything all right?" Dante nearly jumped out of his skin when the guard spoke up.

"Oh, yes," Dante said. "My, um, sister, um, has a headache."

"There's a clinic nearby."

"I see. Thank you."

"You just go down the stairs and turn left."

"Okay," Dante said, thinking, *Please walk away.*

The guard walked away. Dante turned back to the girl.

"I think we need to get you out of here," Dante said. "Where are you headed, anyway?"

"Home?" the girl said, and started crying again.

"You can't ride on the train with your wings unfolded like that."

The girl looked at her hands folded on her lap.

"I live nearby," Dante said. "You can sit in the living room and shake this off or something. You can phone someone to pick you up. Don't you have a phone?"

"It died."

"Let's have it charged, then." Dante smiled. "I'm Dante. What's your name?"

"YOU KNOW I can't tell you my real name," the woman said, firing up a cigarette. She was wearing a short red dress, form-hugging and flattering, and a pair of black pumps with sky-high heels. Waiters came to their table unprompted, bearing extra napkins and glasses and glasses of water. They couldn't stop looking at her. Pauline was amused.

"Of course," Pauline said. "I'm sure you'd like to remain anonymous for the—"

"Diwata don't give you their real names," the woman said. "Every single one of them, every single Diwata you've met and befriended, they've given you fake names. Your name holds enormous power, and to reveal your name is to surrender that power. Back in the days of Lambana I could throw a potent hex at anyone whose real name I knew." She paused. "But then Lambana's been dead for more than a hundred moons now, so why the silly precaution, right? I mean, what's the worse you can do, follow me on Twitter? Old habits die hard, I guess."

She blew smoke out the side of her mouth. "Sorry about that. Bad day at work. Anyway. I've settled with Crystal as my name. Just use C in your article. But you can call me Crystal."

Pauline nodded and added the name to the scribbles on her pad.

"And how is your mother?" Crystal asked.

"A bit worried," Pauline said. Pauline's mother, Ces, was Crystal's boss in the marketing department before Ces was assigned to work in Singapore. During her despedida, she mentioned to Pauline that one of her colleagues had finally decided to have her wings removed. That was five months ago, and Pauline never forgot.

"She thought I'd be mad because she told you I had the operation?" Crystal smirked.

"Are you? Mad, I mean."

Crystal shrugged. "Everyone knows."

"I remember seeing you," Pauline said. "Back when you had them."

"Was I prettier then?"

Pauline laughed, because she didn't know how else to respond.

"You look too young to be working," Crystal said.

"Not too young. I'm nineteen years o—excuse me— about two hundred and thirty moons. This is just freelance work."

"Why this topic?"

"I'm interested." Pauline took out her camera and her digital recorder.

"Interested," Crystal said, in a way that made Pauline feel ashamed. She balanced her cigarette on the ashtray. "I understand you'll need a picture?"

Crystal reached back and zipped down her dress before Pauline could say, "Later." She faced the back of her chair and slipped down one sleeve. Pauline raised her camera and pushed the button. The surgical scar, an open parenthesis before her right scapula, was two handspans long but could very easily be hidden by a concealer. Pauline imagined the waiters looking and scurrying away.

"It's healed well," Pauline said, and helped her zip up.

Crystal resumed smoking her cigarette. "The doctor gave me a cream. It's a bit expensive, but the scar will be invisible in no time. Funny—" she chuckled "—when the news broke that cosmetic surgeons are starting to specialize in wing removal, I was disgusted. Removal! Like they're warts, or an extra finger. Our magic is dead, Lambana is dead, and now they're offering to excise the remaining piece of our identity. I promised myself that I would never, ever, undergo that procedure, unless I'm on the brink of death. Or maybe not even then."

"What made you change your mind?"

"Five months ago I was hurrying to catch the train when my wings suddenly unfolded," Crystal said. "They were mutilated by the train doors. I don't even know how to describe the pain. Diwata wings look so thin and fragile, so I guess most humans think you can just snip them off and you won't feel a thing. But it fucking hurts, I tell you. Like maybe if you had your legs crushed by a car. I passed out, and when I woke up I was in the hospital, and the doctor was telling me I could decide to keep what's left of my wings, but I wouldn't be able to fold them and hide them under my skin anymore, and there could be infections and complications and other shit, so I said 'Doc, let's just remove them.'"

Crystal looked at Pauline and saw the expression on her face. "Your mother didn't tell you the whole story, did she?"

"No, she," Pauline said, flustered. "She said you just decided to have them removed. I thought it was a cosmetic thing. I'm so sorry."

Crystal nodded. "Phantom wings. That's the hardest thing. Every morning you stand up and try to unfold something that isn't there anymore. When it's cold that missing part feels paralyzed, and in the summer that missing part yearns for shade. And the dreams! When I still had my wings I would have flying dreams every now and then, but after the operation I had a flying dream every single night. The exact same dream: one single loop, a view of trees, then I would wake up and feel like it's the end of the world.

"Sometimes I see a group of Diwata who had the cosmetic operation, and I judge them in my head. Fucking hypocrites. Fucking traitors. But like them, I'm wingless now, so what difference does it make? My closest friend also had his wings removed, as a sign of solidarity. We used to fly together. Before the accident we'd often go to Diliman, to that grassy hill overlooking the Athene construction site—you know the place? The one the company abandoned years ago?"

Pauline said, "I know the place."

"We'd go there, late at night, and we'd fly together, relive the old days. But since I can no longer fly, my friend had the operation. Now his is a cosmetic decision, but also a decision borne out of friendship. But what difference does it make?"

"So you regret it?"

"I regret that we are going to die without wings," Crystal said. "You've heard the latest results from the tests. They're all over the news. We're completely barren. We can no longer reproduce. We're the last generation of Diwata, and we have no wings."

"'But have no fear, Sons and Daughters,'" Pauline said, looking at her hands, "'you will rise again—'"

"'—and your wings shall be filled with rain and all the moonlight of your days, and yours will be the glory of Lambana.'" Crystal sighed. "You've read the Book of the Moon. How impressive."

"I saw a translation online," Pauline said. "I hope you don't think I'm being offensive."

"Not at all."

Silence. "I hope the afterlife really is that beautiful," Pauline said.

Crystal's eyes were sad. "Me too," she said. "Me too."

"I SAW A Diwata suddenly take flight along Panay Avenue. He flew so high up so fast he got tangled up in the electric cables."

"You were there?" Pauline said. "I saw that in the news." She was sitting, hugging her knees and chewing her thumbnail, while Mirra lay beside her, an old gray blanket beneath them. Between them a huge flashlight shone a forlorn beam toward the general direction of the Athene construction site, but it was swallowed by darkness before it could even illuminate a single cement block. At least there was a full moon. Pauline was thankful. With the moonlight they could at least see the half-finished columns and the point where they stopped rising from the ground. The utter lack of electric cables.

The sky, dotted with stars, was patient and waiting.

"He died," Mirra said. The dead Diwata could have been her brother, the way her voice sounded. Pauline glanced at her, at Mirra's white top with the lace sleeves and cutoff shorts and dirty Chucks, her wide-open eyes. "His wings and back were burnt to a crisp."

"I know."

"They're saying its urban depression that developed into a full-blown psychotic break." Mirra sighed, lifted her leg, and used the momentum to sit up. Pauline felt a soft breeze against her cheek as Mirra unfolded her wings. "It's sad, isn't it? He just wanted to fly."

"Tell me about Lambana," Pauline said, that night when they first met. Mirra took night classes in the university where Pauline was working on her undergraduate degree, and one dark evening, as Pauline walked to her dorm, she saw a Diwata in a secluded section of the library garden. She had her back to Pauline, one hand holding onto a tree. She was stretching her wings. Pauline stopped, mesmerized. It had been years since she last saw Diwata wings unfolded to their full length. The Diwata's wings shone silver. Pauline had never seen anything like it.

There was a bag with its contents half-spilled on the grass at the Diwata's feet, and Pauline ran to her without thinking.

"Are you okay?" she asked, breathless from the sprint.

"Shit!" the Diwata said, folding her wings in reflex.

"I'm sorry," Pauline said. She gestured to the bag on the ground. "Were you mugged?"

"Almost," the Diwata said, and snatched up her bag. "I slapped him away with my wings."

"Oh, I didn't know you could do that," Pauline said.

"It's a closely guarded secret," the Diwata said, and laughed.

"My name is Pauline." She extended her hand. The Diwata hesitated for a second but eventually shook it. "Maybe you should report what happened to the police. The student council's been asking for more guards for—"

"No," the Diwata said, and shouldered her bag. "I'd rather go home."

"Sorry," Pauline said.

"Or," the Diwata said, "I can go get some tea to calm my nerves. Want to come with?"

"Oh." Pauline said. "Okay." The Diwata had already started walking, and she hurried to catch up with her. "I don't think I caught your name."

The Diwata smiled. "Tea first, darling."

They went to a coffee place on campus. The Diwata brought two cups of hot chai latte to their table. "Tea's on me," she said, "since you took the time to stop and ask how I was back there. Other students wouldn't have spared me a glance."

"It's midterms season," Pauline said, and the Diwata laughed.

"Are you a working student, too? You have a night class?"

"No, I live on campus, I was just on my way back to my dorm. But I do write freelance."

"Nice. I work full-time in a bookstore."

"Oh," Pauline said, and smiled. "I love bookstores."

"The pay's shit," the Diwata said.

They stayed in that corner sipping tea and talking for several hours. Pauline couldn't remember how, but after pretty harmless talk of curriculums and terror profs and the cafeteria on campus that sell egg mayo sandwiches, they ended up talking about the Diwata's dead realm.

"I don't know where that 'iron is poison' bullshit came from," the Diwata said. "Remember that trend, when humans wore iron pendants on a piece of black string? I hated that. It's so silly! Why would anyone think iron can kill us? We mined iron in Lambana."

"I remember that."

"My goodness. But that myth was so widespread. You know they used iron bullets to shoot the Queen."

"They did?" Pauline said. "I thought that was a myth, too."

"Shot the Queen on the field separating the two peaceful realms," she said. "Shot her on the Field of Truce, in the middle of business negotiations."

"Because she spurned a human lover, said the song."

"Another myth," the Diwata said, looking off into the distance and shaking her head. "She was shot because she refused them entrance to the mines. She was shot because the human ambassadors were greedy and she refused to do business with greedy men. In the end the ambassadors got what they wanted. Gold mines and expensive cars. They bled Lambana dry."

Pauline looked into her cup and didn't say anything.

"How did we end up talking about depressing things?" the Diwata said, sensing her discomfort. "Let's talk about egg mayo again."

"Tell me about Lambana," Pauline said. "What do you miss?"

The Diwata closed her eyes and smiled. "Sugar water. Honeyed bread. Flower tea." She opened her eyes. "The smell of the court gardens that no human perfume can ever duplicate. The town square, and how golden it looked in the early morning. The festivals, the dinners after harvest. The dances. The parties. The land was rich enough and our magic effective enough to provide us with all the basic necessities: food, shelter, water, clothing. Most of our days we devoted to sports and the arts, whatever caught our fancy. Magic was used in menial jobs, so no one had to become a menial worker. Everyone was rich and fulfilled. Everyone could afford the luxury to dream."

Her smile faded. "And now I earn minimum wage. I eat fast food almost every day. My cholesterol level is bothering me. I inhale soot. I can't even fly."

"Because of the ordinance?"

"Because of the lack of space!" She held out her arms. "There is no sky in this city. Just wires and cables and billboards and thirty-story buildings." The Diwata dropped her arms and sighed. "I haven't flown in years. I may have flitted from one street to the next, but I haven't flown."

"I'm so sorry," Pauline said.

"I wish I had hoarded gold from Lambana before it fell," the Diwata said. She threw her head back and laughed. Some students turned to look at her.

"You're royalty, aren't you?" Pauline said in a low voice.

The Diwata looked at her with a pleased smile.

"Your wings are silver," Pauline said. "And your eyes—"

"Oh, but this talk of sad things has drained me!" Mirra said. "Come, let us walk you home. Tell a joke on the way, will you?"

Pauline couldn't think of a joke, so the Diwata regaled her with stories of annoying customers at the bookstore. At the dorm, Pauline turned back and said, "Have you heard of the Athene construction site?"

"Is it a bar?"

"I'll bring you there tomorrow," Pauline said. "It's the perfect place for flying. You'll love it."

"Really," the Diwata said with her usual cynical tone, but Pauline could see her visibly containing her excitement.

Pauline nodded. "Good night."

"Mirra."

Pauline turned back with her eyebrows raised.

The Diwata was smiling at her. "My name's Mirra."

"Mirra," Pauline said. "Good night, Mirra."

"PAULINE."

Pauline, yanked out of the past, sat up straighter.

Mirra had mimicked her pose. She was now hugging her knees. "I think I'm sort of scared."

"Do you want to go home now?" Pauline said. In the span of ten months, they had managed to visit the construction site seven times, and each time Mirra got cold feet. "Cold wings," she would say. The first few times Mirra expressed her disappointment in herself through anger: It's been years, why should I even try? And what for? So I can reach the topmost shelf at the store without using a ladder? And why do you care, anyway? Do you really want to help me or do you just want a private show?

Pauline would placate her, and on their commute back Mirra would refuse to meet her eyes. "Why do you even put up with me?" she would say, looking out the window as the aircon of the taxi sputtered and the driver ranted about gas prices.

This time, Mirra didn't respond. She stood up and walked to the edge. She remained that way for what felt like an eternity to Pauline, until Mirra covered her face with her hands and wrapped her wings around her body like a sheet. She was mumbling something. Pauline couldn't understand the words. Mirra lifted her hands to the sky and unfolded her wings. She did this three times. Hands to her face, hands to the sky.

No, she wasn't lifting her hands to the sky, Pauline thought. She was lifting them to the moon.

Mirra jumped.

Pauline gasped. "She did it," she whispered to herself, surprised. "She fucking actually did it." A moment passed.

"Mirra?" Pauline started crawling to the edge on hands and knees, panic settling on her body like dead weight. "Mirra?"

Mirra burst into view, all wings and hair and whoops. Pauline screamed and fell on her side. She could hear Mirra's laughter growing faint as she rose to an impossible height. Then she was swooping down, her breeze on Pauline's skin. "I did it!" she was shouting, eyes as bright as a happy child's. "I did it I did it I did it!"

Mirra flew around the abandoned building for ten minutes. Pauline watched her, itching to take a picture but knowing that she shouldn't. When Mirra's feet touched the ground again, her face was flushed and her hair in disarray, and Pauline could feel her happiness like she would a typhoon, strong as the wind, loud as a thunderstorm.

Mirra embraced her, and Pauline was caught breathless by the impact. She held her hands at her side.

"Thank you," Mirra said, still holding her. Then, amused: "What's the matter?"

"I don't know how to hug you," Pauline said. "Your wings."

"Do it like this," Mirra said, taking her hands, and placed them where they should be.

FOR A CLINIC hidden in a filthy, forgotten strip of stores in Tandang Sora, it was actually quite impressive in its neatness. And Pauline had almost walked away from it. Her source (one of her interviewees who had the surgery, incredibly candid) said this street, this time, behind a massage parlor, but that particular street had eight massage parlors, a fact that her source neglected to mention to her. She couldn't possibly just ask the proprietors one by one if they're hiding an operating room, could she? But in the end, that was what she did. Sort of. She phrased it in a way that wouldn't sound too alarming. *Do you have another store here?*

One or two looked at her through heavy-lidded eyes and said a curt and flat "no", but most responded to the question with frowns and tense backs. "What do you mean do we have another store here?"

Pauline didn't quite know how to respond. "Do you have other services? Do you give manicures or—"

One bored massage therapist raised an eyebrow. "A *special* service? This early?" Her companions erupted in laughter. Pauline felt shame creep up her face, and immediately fled the scene.

The last parlor she walked up to was the parlor she had skipped earlier. She skipped it because she thought it was abandoned. A thick layer of dust covered its tinted windows. Services were written with a felt-tip pen on pieces of cartolina perhaps a decade ago, the cartolina peeling, the ink fading and hardly legible. ONE-HOUR FULL BODY. FOOT MASSAGE. HILOT. SWEDISH. Pauline couldn't make out the prices.

The room was dark and smelled of dead rat and old furniture. There was a man, lanky and young, sleeping behind the front desk. Pauline turned to leave, but the man stirred and said, "Who are you looking for?"

Intrigued, Pauline said, "Dr. Antonio?"

The man pointed to the back of the room and went back to sleep.

Pauline walked past the massage beds and saw a yellowish curtain covering the entire wall. She looked for an opening, felt it, and pushed a portion of the curtain to the side so she could walk through.

Another door. Dark narra, with a generic brass knocker. Pauline lifted the knocker and felt something cut her. She swore. Cheap-ass knockers. She sucked on her finger and, with care, used her other hand to hit the plate twice.

"And who might you be?" a voice said from the other side.

"Vivian sent me here," Pauline said.

The door swung open. The room was air-conditioned, and the ice-cold air hit her square on the face. Dr. Antonio was a tall man in his fifties, wearing square, rimless glasses. He looked trim in a black knitted sweater, white shirt, black pants.

"Vivi!" he said. "She's a hoot and a half, isn't she? Come on in."

The wings were hard to miss. Dr. Antonio (which probably was not his real name, Pauline decided), feeling secure in his nuclear bunk of a clinic, displayed them proudly, vacuum-sealed and backlit in tall glass displays. As if they were merely expensive shoes or designer gowns, and not organs that could easily get him the death penalty. Dr. Antonio stood beside her as she stared, going on and on about wingspan and length and hue. Pauline wondered about the hugeness of the despair that would push a Diwata to sell her own wings. Like the despair a poor father feels before he sells his kidneys. But that need not be the case, right? Life, unlike her view of the world, need not be so melodramatic. If you wanted to have your wings removed anyway, might as well make some cash, right?

"How much did you pay for these?" Pauline asked.

"Oh, so the interview's started?" the doctor said. "Let me make something clear: I agreed to this because I owed Vivian a favor. But you have to understand that you can't divulge my name, or the location of my store. You're going to devastate the non-insured Diwata community if you send me to jail. I think that goes without saying."

Pauline opened her mouth to speak, but the doctor barreled on.

"And I don't trust anyone. In this business, you just can't. We have your name and, I'm afraid, a bit of your blood."

Pauline remembered the knocker.

Dr. Antonio looked apologetic. "You're outraged, I know. It was Vivian's idea. The Diwata have lost their magic, but they can still make potions. So I ask you, please be kind. I don't want to hurt anyone."

"Except mice."

"Excuse me?"

"Vivi has mentioned," Pauline spoke softly, as though the wings could overhear, "that you have experimented with mice. Then cats. Then dogs. That you've given them wings."

Dr. Antonio inhaled and for a second seemed to hold his breath. Pauline waited.

"No," he said in an angry burst. He turned away. "No. Vivi has told you too much, that bitch. No. No, no, no."

"I'm not here to interview you!" Pauline said. The anger in her voice stopped the doctor in his tracks.

Dr. Antonio looked at her, and Pauline felt it. In her head, in her chest. Despair. Its hugeness, its impossible magnitude.

"Please," she said.

"YOU KNOW, YOU'RE not supposed to trust strangers you meet right off the bat, but I'm glad you did. If you'd stayed one minute longer on the platform—" Dante shook his head.

He helped Pauline sit on the couch. She had stopped crying, but looked completely defeated. She sat on the very edge of the couch, treating her wings as if they were glass.

"Relax," Dante said, and handed her a glass of water, which she almost dropped. Dante took out a coaster and placed the glass on the coffee table. "If your back is stiff, your wings will remain stiff. Just relax and they'll fold on their own."

Pauline just looked at him. Her face was ashen.

"Maybe it's wing paralysis," Dante said. He could feel her panic rising like a tide, and tried to think of ways to calm her down. "Don't you think? It happens sometimes when it's about to rain."

The comment snapped Pauline out of her stupor. "You're Diwata?"

"Ah," Dante said, sitting on the coffee table so he could face her. "Well. That depends on your definition."

Pauline frowned, not following.

"I don't have wings anymore," he said. "I had it removed."

"You were injured?" Pauline said.

"No, no. Nothing like that." He smiled, kept his tone light and breezy. The last thing the girl needed, he thought, was a blubbering fool. "I did it for a friend."

Dante had once witnessed a group of construction workers demolish a building with explosives, and he was reminded of this as he watched Pauline's face cave and crumple and fall. She squeezed her eyes shut and cried, howling like a child who had burnt her fingers. Dante wanted to hold her but he could only watch in horror. He wondered what was wrong. Was she in pain? But she sounded as if she were crying for him.

A second later she fell on her stomach on the couch. "Oh dear," Dante said, and fell to his knees. He peered at her face. "What is it?" She was trying to say something, but she was sobbing too hard and couldn't form a coherent word.

"Let me take this off you," Dante said. He stood up and bent over her to remove his jacket.

The back of the jacket was crusty with dried blood. "What—"

And so was the back of her dress, which had absorbed so much blood it looked almost black.

"What," Dante said. His hands were shaking. Dante tried to peel the fabric off her skin. Pauline screamed.

The skin around the roots of Pauline's wings were inflamed and filled with pus. She was bleeding from where her wings joined her body.

"Lambana help me," Dante whispered as he ran around the living room looking for his phone.

"WITH THE MICE and the cats and the dogs I used synthetic wings, of course. With you, if you're absolutely sure you want to volunteer as a test subject, we'll use actual Diwata wings."

"From a dead Diwata?" Pauline shuddered at the thought.

"That's one option. But we'll use wings from a Diwata who decided to have her wings surgically removed. She is of the same height and weight, a perfect match. Of course I'm using the term 'perfect' quite loosely here. We can never be sure of perfect fusion. Wings, like any organ, can be rejected by the recipient body. You have heard of organ rejection, I assume?"

"Of course."

"And of its dangers? This is a major operation, involving nerves and an organ from another species. Fourteen hours on the operating table, a month or more to recover. There will be complications. My experiments with animals were all successful, but they didn't live long.

The mice died after 72 hours. The cats and dogs, after six days."

"You sound like you're trying to dissuade me."

"We've never had a volunteer before. My team and I have only operated on cadavers, figuring out what nerves to fuse with what."

"You should be excited that I'm here, then."

"We'll need you to sign a confidentiality agreement."

"Of course."

"And don't worry. The animals we had allowed to die for the sake of the experiment, but if something goes wrong with your operation, we'll immediately go back in there and remove the organ."

"All right."

"Why are you doing this?"

"Why are *you* doing this?"

"So many Diwata come through my doors wanting to remove the one thing that makes them what they are, and so many humans have so fervently wished to experience flight. There's a niche there."

Pauline forced herself to laugh with him.

"Or," said the doctor, "I have completely lost my mind."

Perhaps I have, too, Pauline thought.

"WHAT THE HELL, Dante, you're not dead. What did you yank me out of my meeting for?"

"Shut the door," Dante said, and pulled Crystal into the apartment.

"Did you kill someone?" Crystal said, and stopped dead in her tracks when she saw the heaving form on the couch.

"This is cruel," Dante said. "This is brutal and malicious and never, never in my entire life—" Dante was too upset to finish his sentence.

"I know this girl," Crystal said. She walked to the couch and called the girl's name. "Pauline?"

"Look at her back."

"Where the hell did you find her?"

"Just look!"

Dante couldn't move Pauline from her position on the couch, so he had covered her with a blanket. Crystal lifted the edge. "Pauline? Pauline, what's wrong?"

Crystal gasped, took three steps back, and fell into a chair. "No," she said.

"You need to call Sean, Crystal."

Crystal didn't reply. She reached into her purse for a cigarette. "Holy mother fucking—" She upended her purse, her lipstick and eyeliner and mascara rolling away, her coins clattering on the floor. She grabbed her packet, shook out a stick, and stuck the cigarette in her mouth. She turned the wheel of her lighter several times but couldn't produce a flame.

"Fennesa!"

Dante, in his panic, had switched to Diwata and called Crystal by her real name.

"Motherfucker!" Crystal said, and threw away her lighter. She banged into the kitchen and banged out again after a few seconds, her cigarette now lit. She took a drag. Inhale, exhale.

"You need to call our doctor!"

"Who would do this," Crystal said. "Who would do this, Dante? Is this a new thing now? Let the Diwata have their wings cut off so they can blend in, then give those wings to humans?"

"Give me Sean's number," Dante said.

"This is unspeakable," Crystal said, pulling out a calling card from her wallet. "This is unforgiveable."

While Dante dialed the number, Crystal sat on the coffee table and touched Pauline's forehead. Her skin was hot to the touch. "Why would you do this, you stupid girl. You are going to kill your mother."

"You think I'm disgusting?" Pauline said.

Crystal took a long drag from her cigarette and expelled the smoke through her nose. She covered her eyes with her left hand and sighed. "Not you, darling. Whoever did this to you. Whoever gave you this option. That's who's disgusting. But why, Pauline? Why would you even—"

"I did it for her," Pauline said through her tears.

"Oh, come *on,*" Crystal said.

"I just wanted to be with her. She said we couldn't be together because I'm not like her. She said we would just fail."

"And you think a pair of wings was the answer?"

"She flies and I'm left behind," Pauline said. "It hurts that there's a place she can go to and I can't follow."

"Sean is on his way!" Dante called from Crystal's room. "I'll go pack some of your old clothes so Pauline can have something to change into at the hospital!"

"I understand what you mean," Crystal said to Pauline, and held her hand. "You're crazy, but I understand what you mean."

"It was supposed to be a surprise," Pauline said, crying. "But something went wrong. I was fine when I left the clinic. I was supposed to get on the train but my wings wouldn't fold. They offered a car. I should have just taken the car."

"You'll be okay."

"It was supposed to be a surprise." Pauline cried.

"What was her name?" Crystal asked.

"Diwata don't give their real names."

"I'm afraid so. What name did she give you, then?"

"She told me to call her Mirra," Pauline said. "She has silver wings."

Crystal looked stunned. "Dante?" she called, but Dante was busy packing.

"Mirra," Pauline repeated. The girl looked at her through heavy lids. "Mirra. That's her name."

Crystal patted her hand. "She must really like you, dear," she said, "because that girl gave you her real name."

I'M SORRY.

Can you please forgive me? Can we talk?

Talk to me, please.

All the permutations. It was five in the morning and Mirra couldn't sleep. For more than a month she'd been sending texts and emails. The girl at the dorm said Pauline had filed a leave of absence and wouldn't be back until the next semester. Mirra didn't know what that meant. She had nothing but a single email that said: *I'll go away for a while, but I'll come back and I'll be perfect for you. Please don't give up on me.*

Please talk to me.

I regret what I said.

Please forgive me.

Can you still forgive me?

Mirra still couldn't find the right words. She swung away from her computer monitor, put her face in her hands.

Her phone was ringing. An unknown number. *Maybe that's why I'm not getting a reply,* Mirra thought, *because she's changed her number! Maybe—*

Hope, against her will, blossomed in her chest. She grabbed her phone and answered.

"I THINK THAT girl had a mental breakdown," Dante said.

Crystal yawned. She shook another cigarette out of her packet. "I think that girl was in love," she said, firing up. "But yes, same difference."

Sean, acclaimed doctor to the Diwata ("And pretty soon," he always said, "to the stars"), had driven Pauline to St. Luke's and used a different entrance, already hell-bent on keeping things quiet. Surgery took ten hours, and Crystal and Dante slept in one cot in an empty room, the first time they had done so since they were moonlings. Dante had insisted on sleeping on the floor so Crystal could have the bed to herself, but it had been a crazy day and Crystal wanted to hold someone close.

Significant blood loss, extensive nerve damage, danger of sepsis, under observation—they couldn't quite understand the words, but they all sounded bad.

"Not to worry, though," Sean told them before shooing them away. "The girl's holding on. She's actually doing well, considering her injuries. She'll pull through. This one's a fighter."

"You're going to write a paper on her, aren't you?" Dante said.

"You bet your cute ass I am."

Crystal called to tell Pauline's mother that her daughter had been in an accident. She wanted to call another number but Dante insisted that they go out and get some fresh air. He hated hospitals.

They found themselves on the hill overlooking the Athene construction site, their favorite spot. Crystal smoked her cigarette.

"Again with the love angle," Dante said.

"I know what she told me."

"She was delirious!"

"How could she have known Princess Mirra's name?" Crystal said. "And the fact that the Princess has silver wings?"

"That girl's practically a Diwata scholar," Dante said. "You told me she knew the Book of the Moon. She'd know what the royals look like."

"And the Princess's name? That was never divulged. I only knew the name of the Queen's children after Lambana fell, and no one was writing any books then."

Dante fell silent.

"There's an 'M' in her phonebook," Crystal said. "I copied the number. We could call her—"

"And ask her to open the doorway to Lambana?"

"Yes!" Crystal said.

"Okay, let's say we do find the Princess," Dante said. "What if she refuses? What if you get to talk to her, and the Princess refuses?"

"Well, she'd be the biggest bitch if she did," Crystal said. "But it's worth a shot."

"Why are you being Miss Positivity all of a sudden?"

"And why are you being so negative?" Crystal said. "We need hope, okay? Maybe it's false hope, maybe it's the kind of hope that will destroy us in the end, but we need it. We have no magic, we can never have children, the bloodline stops with us. And now we can't even fly!"

"Oh, Crystal."

"I'm so sorry I was stupid enough to have my wings destroyed by train doors, stupid enough to let you go through that operation, you idiot. But maybe the new Queen can give us back our wings! Who knows?"

Dante held her hand.

"Crystal," he said.

Crystal started to cry. Dante watched her, mute and helpless.

"Let's call her," Dante said.

Crystal didn't react. She kept crying.

"The Princess. Let's call her."

It took a moment for Dante's words to sink in. "Oh," Crystal said, and wiped away her tears. "Really?"

"Like you said—it's worth a shot."

Crystal smiled. She took her phone out of her pocket and put the call on loudspeaker.

"It's ringing," Crystal said. She placed her phone on the ground, and they put their heads together and watched the blinking screen closely as if it were a sacred artifact.

"Remember the first time we found this place?" Dante said, nervous and wanting to mask his nervousness with idle chatter. He looked at the mounds of cement, the rusty scaffoldings, the building, unfinished and abandoned. Everything was ugly except the sky, now black, now purple, now lilac, now rose.

Crystal held him close. "I remember," she said. They leaned against each other, buoyed by the memory of flight, and waited for the call to connect.

LET ME HOLD YOUR HAND

I use the word *place*, encircled several times in an academic article on Pierre Bourdieu, coupling it with *longing*, highlighted in an Adrienne Rich poem printed on the back of what looks like a grocery list. More words to figure out, but later, later. This is a trial. Let me see how I go on my first attempt. I scratch the words on my own front door, which swings out not to an empty hallway but a sitting area in a flower garden, cool, secluded, the wooden bench overrun with vines I can't name.

There's only a handful of steps from the door to the bench. I sit down. A mirror appears in mid-air. Superimposed on my face are the ghostly wisps of what looks like a ship. No, tentacles; alien limbs growing out of my cheeks and forehead. After a few seconds, they disappear, and I end up just looking at my own face.

Not the right words, then.

THERE ARE SIXTEEN books and eighteen folders of paper—stapled, folded together, loose odds and ends—in the box your parents have sent me. Three of the books—*The Distance to Andromeda and Other Stories*, *Sa Mil Flores*, *May Isang Hostes*, and *The Little Prince*—have copious notes written in the margins. I can't understand the marginalia. They are written in a script I can hardly read. The letters—or syllables, or words—resemble hiragana or baybayin.

I feel like finding the right words to enter will take me forever.

Is this your intention?

I KNOW YOU enjoy collecting trivia. I find one that you've scribbled in the margins of a Tokyo itinerary:

> *Did you know that hiragana was developed by*
> *women during Japan's Heian era, and was distrusted*
> *by men because official documents at the time*
> *were still written using Chinese characters?*

I carve *translate* into the door to the kitchen, but unlike my first attempt, the door just opens to the kitchen, the word unable to unlock anything at all.

I KNOW YOU didn't use the Latin alphabet, but you can't fault me for being desperate.

I look through the book's margins again. My head is starting to throb from the pain of trying to remember a long-forgotten language.

IN 2001, CANADIAN linguist Sonja Lang created Toki Pona, a language with a really small vocabulary—it only has 120 words. A single word would have multiple meanings. The word *ike*, for example, means "bad, evil, complex and unnecessary".

In order to express yourself, you have to be both creative and direct. You can combine the words to say something new, infuse it with your own perspective, describe the world through metaphor.

Mi ike.

I am bad/evil/complex/unnecessary.

I HAVE A co-worker who would talk at length about the various K-pop bands she loves and whoever the golden maknae and her bias is in each band—whatever those terms meant.

I wish I have that, that passion that makes you talk with excitement even with a co-worker you hardly know, that buoy you up every day.

I work in office admin now. Lots of work but relatively low stress because I don't need to make big decisions. I take lunch orders, I buy the cake for staff birthdays, I file documents, I refill the office pantry with paper plates and coffee beans. There are days when I can work from nine in the morning until five in the afternoon with minimal human interaction, my mind filled with nothing but static, white noise. Those are the good days.

I like being busy because when I'm not busy I end up thinking about what happened to us and to you, especially, and I don't like thinking about that. I once washed all the dishes—dirty *and* clean—in the pantry by hand just to keep myself occupied. I often drink myself to sleep because it takes me a long time to fall asleep and I can't stand it. I can't stand it. The thoughts sit with me like unwelcome guests and I need to keep them out and make sure they stay out however I can.

THIS ISN'T SUSTAINABLE. I know. The one time I decided to share a personal story to someone in the office, it ended in disaster.

One of my co-workers was talking about his upcoming climb, and I interrupted him to say that on my last hiking trip (you know which one), we passed by two boys coming down the mountain. They were local residents selling goods at the campsite before the summit, returning to lowland to get more canned drinks at the town store. Good morning, the group leader said, and we followed suit, greeting the boys as they moved down the line. Good morning! the boys said. Good morning! Good morning!

I heard that while hiking you need to greet every person you meet, I told my co-worker. You know why?

To be polite? he said.

No, I said. To make sure they're human.

I felt antsy, as I had back then. I remember brushing this feeling away as the anxiety of a city-dweller, unused to nature, to little animals watching your every move.

Okay, he said, laughing, and my co-workers looked at each other as if I were a statue that had come to life.

I was holding my water bottle at the time, and I turned and threw it as hard as I could at the window.

I don't know why. I'm thinking now that maybe if I didn't throw it at the window I would have thrown it at his face.

I'm sorry, I wanted to say in the stunned silence that followed as glass shards fell to the floor. I didn't mean to. I could see people from the other departments popping their heads in to see what had happened. I could feel shame burning like a molten ball in my chest.

One of the older ladies in the office walked over to me, placed her hand on my shoulder, and asked, to my surprise, if I was okay. I blinked away tears, and just like that, I was angry again, swiping at her hand, screaming at her to leave me alone.

Why do I always feel like this, like the attacker and the victim at the same time?

You and I entered a seam in the fabric of the universe, but why didn't it change me? I was like this before we entered and I'm still like this even after we left. Why didn't it make me better?

SO I WAS asked to take a few days off, and the boxes of books came from your parents, and now here I am, with all the time in the world to think and think and think.

HERE'S ANOTHER TRIVIA for you:

Did you know that there is such a thing as an "autonomous language"? It's a private, secret language invented by two children, often twins, who grow up together. A language different from the language spoken in their environment, and which only they can understand.

In 1963, two twins, isolated from society, made a pact to only speak their language to one another, a pact that they held until one of the twins died in 1993. That year, the surviving twin began to speak English again.

We're not twins, but what else could bring two people closer than to be lost in time?

ONCE THERE WERE two young people trapped beneath the open sky for what felt like centuries, and while one of them spiralled deeper into despair, the other found courage within herself and created a new language. A lexicon composed of a few dozen pictographic symbols constructed out of boredom or desperation because really what else was there left to do.

OUT OF NOWHERE I remember your word for *fire*.

It makes sense for it to be the first to surface in my memory, being the symbol we've had to use many, many times, in that Nowhereplace, the In-Between, the Neither-Here-Nor-There with no shelter, no respite.

I take one of your old papers and draw the symbol on the margin. Like alien limbs growing out of a circle.

The sheet immediately bursts into flame.

I scream, fall to the floor.

The paper has turned into ashes.

Your words remain potent. If only I can remember the rest.

WHAT I REMEMBER:
  • the symbol for *friend* is an oval with two dots inside, like a face
  • *friend* plus *fire* means *anger*
  • *friend* plus *water* means *sorrow*

Your symbol for *water* looks like a ship. You said you chose this because you can't swim, but you like ships. You once went on a cruise with your father when you were nine, and you said sitting on a ship that large made you feel as if you weren't on water at all. As if the ocean did not exist.

I remember the first door I opened. The garden with the mirror. The tentacles growing out of my face, the ghostly shape.

Sorrow.

Is that what you want to say?

Or is that what I want to say.

IN ONE OF our last conversations, back when you were still lucid, do you remember what you said to me?

You said I should talk to someone, and I said, I'm talking to you.

And you said, I can't handle everything for you I can't comfort you and hold your hand all the time I did that over there and it's not easy I get sad and scared too so if I'm sad or scared who do I turn to who is there for me—

THE OLDER LADY in the office, the one who asked how I was after my outburst? Her name is Madeline. She's in her fifties, a widow, mother of two, and she reached out to me via email during my forced leave or suspension or whatever you want to call it. She says I remind her of her daughter. I don't know if that's a good thing or a bad thing. She says to email her back whenever, if I want to sit down for a chat.

Look, I've never had counselling before. Therapy requires honesty and I can't really be completely honest. During our hiking trip, I was gone for fifteen minutes and you were gone for an hour. The hiking group was only mildly concerned until they found us filthy and emaciated. We were in whatever that place was for years. It was *years*. Until now, I still sleep on the floor of my apartment because sleeping on a soft surface feels strange, unnatural. How can I even begin to explain this to anyone? You were the only one I can truly talk to about it, but you were right, you can't handle everything for me, you're sick of being reminded of what we went through, so I stopped talking to you. You were able to move on much faster than I did even though I was the one who got out of there first.

SO EMAILING MADELINE back was the next best thing.

We agreed to meet online. When I logged on, my face and hair were superimposed like a ghost over Madeline's face. Madeline is bright and bubbly. On our call, she was wearing red earrings shaped like strawberries and her smile was open and warm, with no hint of a shadow behind it at all.

I needed to couch my story in terms that she would understand, so this was what I told her:

I have this recurring dream.

There's this friend that I first met years ago on a hike.

During the hike (*in the dream*, I emphasized) we get lost.

We end up in a section of the forest that's not part of the trail.

Somehow we can't get out.

Have you seen *Survivor*? That place is like that, except there's no camera crew to help us out, no medic, no million-dollar prize at the end. We have to build a lean-to from whatever branches we can find so we can have shelter. Luckily we have provisions in our backpacks, but eventually we have to make our own fire, boil our water, hunt for food.

In the dream (I emphasized again), we stay in that place for what feels like a really long time.

Eventually my friend becomes convinced that there is a way out of there, she just needs to find the right word. She picks up twigs and writes into the soil, trying to find the right word that would give us a way out.

Then one day, while gathering branches for the fire, I meet someone else. She looks like a woman, but I know she isn't human. She is very beautiful. She is wearing a white shift dress, with long black hair up to her waist, intense eyes. She sits on the massive roots of a tree and gestures for me to come closer.

She says she's the guardian of the place, and once people trespass they can't leave.

I tell her we're not trespassing, we just got lost.

She says my friend is trying to tap into the enchantment of this place. She doesn't seem to like that.

She says she'll let me go if I tell her what my friend is trying to do to escape.

I tell her that she should just let both of us go.

She says if I don't tell her now, she won't give me another chance.

So.

I tell her.

I don't even stop to think about it. It surprises me, how easily I betray my friend.

I tell her about the symbols my friend is constructing, about her plans.

I tell the guardian: Is this a test? If this is a test, I have failed it, haven't I?

She doesn't respond after that, but she holds up her end of the bargain. She lets me go. I turn around and suddenly there's a path in front of me, the familiar undergrowth, the sound of bamboo creaking in the wind. But my friend gets stuck there for a while longer.

I think it ruined her life. I think I ruined her life.

Then Madeline asked: In the dream?

What?

In the dream? Or are you saying you think you ruined her life for real?

It took me a moment to get my bearings.

Madeline said: How is your friend now? Are you still in touch?

She died last week.

Oh.

I only found out because her parents sent her boxes of books to me. They said she wanted me to have them. Before she passed, my friend was diagnosed with early-onset dementia. She started losing her words. Profound word-finding difficulty, the doctors said. After about a year, she had to resort to pointing at objects because she couldn't remember what something was called.

How terrible. I am truly sorry.

My friend tells me (*in the recurring dream I have, I emphasized*) that there must be a way to slice off a piece of reality, carve a small pocket of the universe that will remain unchanged. I imagine it's like an eternal room I can visit, if I knew the right word to open the door. In this room, my friend waits with all of her words and all of her memories still intact, and she's healthy and happy and not wasting away on a bed because she's lost her appetite and no longer wants to eat. Did you know that in the end stages of dementia, the disease affects the part of your brain that controls swallowing? Did you know that? I never knew that.

Madeline fell silent, watching me cry. I kind of wondered if she was enjoying this. I sat with growing resentment. I just kept thinking: What am I even doing here? This person can't help me. She thinks I'm just talking about a dream. Sooner or later she will ask the dreaded questions: What do you think this dream means? What do you think the guardian symbolizes? Believing the signifier is not the signified.

And you want to see your friend again? Madeline said.

Of course! I was shouting. I was angry now. I wanted to throw my laptop against the wall. Of course, I want to see my friend again.

Madeline asked: Do you blame yourself for what happened to your friend?

When I didn't answer, she said: You must know that you didn't cause her to have dementia.

This made me even angrier. How can she be so sure? I don't know what that place is, what it can do to you, and I left you there alone.

Sometimes we like having someone to blame, Madeline continued. Even if that someone is ourselves. We find comfort in finding answers. It's how we find meaning in tragedy.

I asked her how come I'm not comforted, if that's true.

Madeline didn't answer for a long time. Then she said: Think about how you want to honor your friend's life.

I FALL ASLEEP after my chat with Madeline and
actually have a dream about you.

The door swings open and there's the sitting area
again, the flower garden.

I sit down and I see your face in the mirror,
superimposed on my face like a ghostly reflection.

You climb out of the mirror as if it were a window
and sit on the wooden bench next to me.

We never did reach the summit, didn't we? you say.

No, I say. We got lost, remember?

I look down and I'm wearing my hiking gear: sturdy
shoes, leggings, a moisture-wicking shirt.

This is a do-over, you say.

We both stand up, carrying our backpacks. We walk
away from the garden to the start of the trail. Someone
from the hiking group named Mike asks the participants
to gather round for a group photo before the ascent. Most
of the hikers come in groups: friends, colleagues, a set of
siblings. I stand next to you, another young woman hiking
solo.

Mike talks about the trail, the rugged terrain, the
continuous ascent. There are two summits, and he gives
a firm reminder that no one will be forced to reach either
summit against their will.

The trail to the summit of Mt. Palay-Palay has no
trees or twigs, so you need to literally crawl your way
up on dusty soil. The monolith is a steep climb at 90
degrees—Mike gestures with his arms—so you'll need to
rappel.

Nervous, giddy laughter.

The ascent to the summit of the monolith is very challenging, so we ask you, especially the women, not to push through to the second summit if you think you can't do it.

Especially the women? you echo, and I wince as I did that day.

This smug jerk, you say. What's his name again? *Mike?*

All I know is that Mike is in for a world of hurt.

I'm the Group Leader, Mike says, and Jeremy is our Group Sweeper, which means he will stay at the back of the group to keep count, and accompany whoever may be lagging behind. Again, no pressure! Your health and well-being is more important to us than reaching the summit.

Especially if you have a vagina, I say, which makes you snicker.

Is this the moment we have decided that we should become friends?

Some members of the group keep chatting as we walk, but I focus on my breathing and stare at my shoes, only looking up when you say, Look at these trees! The trees tower over us, buttress roots nearly reaching our waists.

The beginning of the trail is easy enough since we are walking on level land, but once the ascents begin, some of them so steep we have to climb hand-over-hand over tangled roots, I find myself quickly running out of breath. We stop several times to sit down, drink water, recuperate. The final rest stop before the summit of Mt. Palay-Palay opens up to a view of Pico de Loro, the second summit shaped like a parrot's beak.

In the dream, I stop.

We never saw this.

The campsite is a huge clearing where hikers can lie down on the grass, or buy food and beverage from the makeshift sundry stores erected by the residents. It offers an amazing view of the two summits. Out here, in the sunlight, every color stands out. The green of the mountain and the blue sky hurt my eyes. I sit on the grass, a towel covering my head, and watch a group attempt a jump shot. A dragonfly, red and plump, sits on my knee, and I wonder idly how this insect can fly so high. The other hikers are eating the lunch they packed, sharing food around on paper plates. You remain standing, hands on hips, shuffling your feet. I can feel you looking at me, like a cook waiting for a pot to boil.

Are you okay? you ask. I can get you food if you like.

I draw the towel to my face and burst into tears. Your hand is on my nape. Don't be kind to me. Please. I don't deserve it.

Can we go to the summit now? you say. It's a shame. It's right there, and we came all this way.

The sun burns my arms, and the barren soil in which I try to find purchase burns my fingers. Soon the summit comes, and the hikers resting on top of Mt. Palay-Palay cheer when we emerge. You place an arm around me, shaking me gently.

We did it!

I'm sorry, I say. I'm so sorry.

I don't think you hear me. You're already on your way to the second summit, scaling the monolith, eager to prove stupid Mike wrong.

I see you on the summit, alone, cheering and raising your hands to the sky.

I GO BACK to my front door and scratch out *place* and *longing* and carve the symbols for *friend* and *water*. *Sorrow*. This is all I've been feeling for years. Can't this be the word to lead me back to you? But I open the door and there's only the empty hallway.

IN THE LANGUAGE you constructed, to write *forgiveness* you need to combine the symbols for *friend* and *knowledge*.

How can you forgive me if you can't even remember me, if you don't even know what I did?

But maybe this is my penance, to continue to remember for the both of us. Maybe there is no door that will open for me, and all I can do is live in this room with no exit.

WHEN WE LAST spoke, you said that we should be lucky to only lose fifteen minutes, or one hour, that there's more life for us to live. Move on, you said. At the time, you didn't know what was going to happen to you, and I never got the chance to confess that whatever was guarding that place gave me a way out if I betrayed you. And I betrayed you, just like that.

How can I move on, knowing all this?

I wish, with all my heart, that you've managed to carve a small pocket in space and time. That's the only way to make any of this fair.

I hope you'll visit me in my dreams again and let me know you're all right where you are.

HOW CAN I honor your life?

Last night I dreamt that I was leading a hiking trip, and that I was happy. I was the resilient, strong-willed person I always wished I could have been to you, someone you could depend on, with no worries in the world, focused on the one goal ahead. Soil, sun, sky, mountain, the laughter of friends, my body taking it all in—this was all, this was all that was left, and what a blessed life to only want this and have this and nothing else.

An Eighteenth Prayer

Realizing that this volume comes out a full decade
after the release of *A Bottle of Storm Clouds* (2012),
my first short story collection and my first published
book, fills me with awe and gratitude. (And
perhaps a tinge of melancholy, knowing that time
can go by so, so fast and that each writer really,
truly, only has a handful of books within them).
I would like to thank my family, friends, editors,
and avid readers for their love and support through
the years. If the Many-Eyed Mother can accept
an eighteenth prayer, I would pray for your joy,
health, and safety for the many decades to come.

Nida Ramirez is family, friend, editor, and
avid reader rolled into one ~ my deepest
thanks for taking on *Storm Clouds* and
kickstarting all this exciting craziness.

This book is for my best friend and
constant companion, Jaykie.

Eliza Victoria
March 2022

The following stories first appeared, at times in earlier versions, in the following publications:

- "Fairy Tales." *Daily Science Fiction*, June 8, 2012. Reprinted in *Chasing Tales: Vol 1, Fantasy Night* by MoarBooks in 2014.
- "The Missing." *Maximum Volume: Best New Filipino Fiction 2014*, February 28, 2014.
- "1:40 AM." *Daily Science Fiction*, August 8, 2014.
- "Deliver Us." *Philippine Speculative Fiction 9*, October 9, 2014.
- "The Seventh." *Likhaan: The Journal of Contemporary Philippine Literature*, November 2015. Reprinted in the *Apex Book of World SF Volume 5* in 2019.
- "Fortitude." *Science Fiction: Filipino Fiction for Young Adults*, May 2016. Reprinted in *POC Takes Over Fantastic Stories of the Imagination*, 2017.
- "Premium." *Let's Eat (Special Fiction issue): Philippine Star*, June 26, 2016.
- "Queen Midnight." *The Dark*, May 1, 2017.
- "The Impossible Place." *Theme of Absence*, April 13, 2018.
- "Carpe Noctem." *LONTAR: The Journal of Southeast Asian Speculative Fiction*, May 2018.
- "After the Crash," *Philippine Speculative Fiction Volume 11*, July 11, 2018.
- "A Prayer to the Many-Eyed Mother." *The Dark*, September 2018.

• "Ayani." *Stranded: Lone Survivor Deserted Island Horror Stories*, Dark Regions Press, October 2018.
• "Where you are now is better than where you were before." *Fireside Fiction*, October 2019.

"The Ghosts of Sinagtala" originally appeared in *Unseen Moon*, which had a limited print run in 2013.

"When I die, I want you to have all of my stuff" was originally an interactive story self-uploaded and hosted on *Philome.la* in 2014.

"Fairy Tales" was written before *After Lambana*, which to me now reads like a prequel to "Fairy Tales". This was not how the story was originally conceived, but for the sake of narrative consistency, I have re-written the version of "Fairy Tales" that appears here as a sequel to *After Lambana*, keeping it in line with the lore and history presented in the graphic novel. The plot remains largely the same, so if you've read the original version, there are no big surprises.

"Let Me Hold Your Hand." *Daata*, March 2022. Commissioned by Daata as part of the 2022 Art Fair Philippines exhibition *Aparisyon* with artist Leeroy New.
• For more information about Toki Pona, visit https://tokipona.org/

• The translation of "ike" as "bad, evil, complex, unnecessary" is from https://devurandom.xyz/tokipona/1.html an unofficial Toki Pona guide created by /dev/urandom

• The twins mentioned in this story are based on June and Jennifer Gibbons, as discussed by linguist Ben Macaulay here https://gizmodo.com/whats-the-newest-language-1847750011

• *The Distance to Andromeda and Other Stories* (1960) is a book written by Gregorio Brillantes. *Sa Mil Flores, May Isang Hostes at iba pang kwento* (2015) is a book by Rosario de Guzman-Lingat. Antoine de Saint-Exupéry's *The Little Prince* was first published in English in 1943.

• Mt. Palay-Palay is also known as Mt. Pico de Loro, and is located in Cavite in Central Luzon, Philippines. Palay-Palay/Pico de Loro was closed to hiking activities from 2016 to 2019 for rehabilitation purposes.

ELIZA VICTORIA *is the author of several books including the*
Philippine National Book Award-winning Dwellers,
the novel Wounded Little Gods, *the graphic novel*
After Lambana *(a collaboration with Mervin Malonzo),*
and the science fiction novel-in-stories, Nightfall.
She has won prizes in the Philippines' top literary awards,
including the Carlos Palanca Memorial Awards for Literature.
Her one-act plays, written in Filipino, have been staged at
the Virgin LabFest at the Cultural Center of the Philippines.
Dwellers, Wounded Little Gods, *and* After Lambana *were*
released worldwide by Tuttle Publishing in 2022.
Visit her at elizavictoria.com

9 786218 264113